Also by
Lynn Weingarten

Suicide Notes from Beautiful Girls

bad
girls
with
perfect
faces

Lynn Weingarten

SIMON PULSE
New York London Toronto Sydney New Delhi

SIMON PULSE

An imprint of Simon & Schuster Children's Publishing Division

1230 Avenue of the Americas, New York, New York 10020

First Simon Pulse hardcover edition October 2017

Text copyright © 2017 by Lynn Weingarten

Jacket photograph copyright © 2017 by Ashraful Arefin/Arcangel Images

All rights reserved, including the right of reproduction in whole or in part in any form.

SIMON PULSE and colophon are registered trademarks of Simon & Schuster, Inc.

For information about special discounts for bulk purchases, please contact Simon & Schuster Special Sales at 1-866-506-1949 or business@simonandschuster.com.

The Simon & Schuster Speakers Bureau can bring authors to your live event.

For more information or to book an event contact the Simon & Schuster Speakers Bureau at 1-866-248-3049 or visit our website at www.simonspeakers.com.

Jacket designed by Regina Flath

Interior designed by Tom Daly

The text of this book was set in Adobe Caslon Pro.

Manufactured in the United States of America

2 4 6 8 10 9 7 5 3 1

Library of Congress Cataloging-in-Publication Data

Names: Weingarten, Lynn, author.

Title: Bad girls with perfect faces / by Lynn Weingarten.

Description: First Simon Pulse hardcover edition. | New York : Simon Pulse, 2017. |

Summary: Seventeen-year-old Sasha, desperate to save her best friend Xavier from more heartache, creates a social media trap for his ex-girlfriend with the hopes of exposing her cheating ways, but Sasha's plan takes a dangerous turn that dramatically changes the course of everyone's life.

Identifiers: LCCN 2017015886 (print) | LCCN 2017030007 (eBook) |

ISBN 9781481418621 (eBook) | ISBN 9781481418607 (hardcover)

Subjects: | CYAC: Best friends—Fiction. | Friendship—Fiction. | Social media—Fiction.

Classification: LCC PZ7.W43638 (eBook) | LCC PZ7.W43638 Bad 2017 (print) |

DDC [Fic]—dc23

LC record available at https://lccn.loc.gov/2017015886

bad
girls
with
perfect
faces

Sasha

We were holding hands, palm against palm. I could feel his heart beating, his blood against my blood.

When I looked up, his smile was wide and real. "Ready?" he said.

I faked a smile back. I had gotten so good at faking things.

I thought: *You brought this on yourself, Sasha. You will never get to stop pretending.*

I thought: *Protect those you love, no matter what the cost.*

He squeezed my hand. This is exactly what I always wanted. And nothing I ever wanted at all. And there is just no taking anything back.

"Let's go," I said.

"Road trip!" he said.

He couldn't begin to imagine what this actually was. He had no idea what I'd done. What any of us had.

I turned the key. The engine started. We went.

Part I

Sasha

3 weeks, 1 day earlier

On the eve of Xavier's seventeenth birthday, I decided I was finally going to tell him the truth.

We were in his bathroom with a folding chair pushed up against the sink and I was dyeing his hair as his birthday present.

"I want it to look like a very deep part of the ocean," he'd said a few days earlier, when he'd asked me to do it. "Like something a whale would drink."

I'd taken this as a good sign: him wanting something, expressing wanting something. He'd spent the last month in his room wanting nothing but quiet and to sleep, or maybe his ex-girlfriend back, though we mostly didn't talk about that part.

"The ocean isn't any color," I'd said. "It's just water."

"Then like the bottom of the ocean if somebody dumped a whole bunch of blue food coloring in it."

I bought the bleach and a bottle of dye that looked like ink. I also got a bag of Swedish Fish, because that was our favorite candy, and it worked with the whole ocean theme. We were both really into the ocean back then.

I put the bleach on his hair while he sat on the chair. I had to lean in to do it, and that made my heart pound, and then I felt guilty for its pounding, because it was messed up to feel that way about him and be that close without him knowing. *But I'll tell him soon*, I promised myself. *I will tell him, and it won't be a secret anymore.*

The bleach burned our eyes and our noses as it turned his hair from black to coppery gold, and then from coppery gold to almost white. We drank whisky and ate the candy and watched part six of the eight-part ocean documentary series we'd been working our way through on his laptop. This episode was about whales and how sometimes a whale will go years in between seeing any other whales. It just floats along down there in the dark, all alone. "Well, that doesn't sound so bad," Xavier said. But I knew he didn't mean it.

After the bleach, I put on the dye. Xavier had already thrown away the plastic gloves, and so I got the blue all over my hands, and then it wouldn't come off. "Oh my God, I'm so sorry," he said when he saw what had happened. But he was laughing, which meant it was worth it.

We poured more whisky into our mugs and clinked them.

The buzzer on my phone went off, it was time to rinse. "I'll get in the shower," Xavier said. I got up and started to leave the bathroom, and he said, "No, just turn around." But it felt very wrong to be in there while he was taking his clothes off, considering, even if I wasn't looking. "I'll go wait in your room," I said. "So the steam won't mess up my hair." The water was already on, and loud.

And he shouted, "Since when do you care about steam on your hair?"

"People change!" I shouted back.

I sat on his bed and stared down at my blue hands and decided enough was enough was enough was enough. I wouldn't just tell him soon, I would tell him *tonight*. But how would I say it? I'd tried to imagine a million times but had never quite come up with the words. *Xavier, I know this might sound like it's coming out of nowhere, but . . .* or *Xavier, you know how I always say I don't want to date anyone, well the thing is . . .* Maybe it would be better not to plan. Maybe it would be better to just be brave: take a deep breath, open my mouth, and let my heart climb right out of it.

A few minutes later he came into his room in a towel, and I pretended to need to use the bathroom. When I got back he was standing there . . . dressed.

"What do you think?" he said. His hair hung in thick wet clumps. The blue was way lighter than it was supposed to be, like jeans that had been washed a thousand times. "I haven't even looked yet," he said. "I waited for you."

He bit his lip and opened his eyes wide, a caricature of a nervous person waiting for a reaction. My face grew hot—he was beautiful. How strange to remember that I actually used to find him very ordinary looking. It seemed impossible to me now.

"Oh God, your expression. Is it bad? It's bad." He went over to the mirror. Xavier was not someone who looked in the mirror a lot. It was possible he hadn't even seen himself in a month.

"No, it's good," I said.

He ran his hands through his hair, frowned, smiled, made a duck face, made a fish face. "Are you sure?" he said.

"Stop fishing," I said. "That's a command and also an ocean joke."

He grinned. "I guess it's time to be a functional human being and go out somewhere?" he said. "Like you've been saying all along? For my, like, birthday or something?"

It was the first time he had wanted to go out in a month.

He poured some more whisky into one of the mugs I'd made for him at the print-and-copy shop where I worked. This one had a picture of him holding a mug with a picture of him holding a mug with a picture of him holding a mug on it.

I thought maybe he was pouring too much whisky, considering. "Don't worry," he said, watching me watching him. "I promise this is okay." He motioned to the whisky. "I'm really not going crazy like that anymore."

It was almost eight thirty. Through the window, the sun was setting and the sky was pink and red. "Well, we should at least have some snacks if we're going to drink like this," I said.

I went to his kitchen and grabbed some string cheese and pita chips. I told him to open the chips and cheeses and eat them, and we made a game of me directing him around. "Pull off a string. Put it in your mouth. Chew, chew, chew," I said. "Now swallow."

"Isn't it weird, because string cheese is not really string and not really cheese and yet somehow is both?" he said.

"Save it for open-mic night, pal," I said. "And keep eating."

He opened up the pita chips. "Pita chips, neither pita nor chip!" he said.

I rolled my eyes. "Shoe yourself," I said. "Become shod." And I pointed to his Converse on the floor.

"Are you going to make all my decisions for me tonight?" he said.

"We'll see," I said.

"About time someone reasonable took over."

We had another gulp of whisky each, then poured the rest into an empty Cherry Coke bottle, and it was time to go.

We walked to the train station. "Left foot, right foot, left foot, right foot," I said. We passed the bottle back and forth. The air outside was warm and soft. It was dark now.

The platform was mostly empty. Xavier and I leaned up

against the wall. Our arms were touching. *Now kiss me*, I thought, but didn't say it.

The train pulled up, we got on. We drank and drank while the trees rushed by outside. An old man was glaring at us over the top of his newspaper, and staring at my blue hands, which I'd forgotten about. Because I was a little bit drunk, I held my hands up like claws and bared my teeth at him. The man just shook his head.

"Thanks for being the world's best friend," Xavier said. "I love you."

I turned toward the window, I felt my face getting hot. "I didn't say speak," I said.

He clamped his hand over his mouth.

"That's more like it."

But what I was thinking about was the last time he'd told me he loved me, eleven days before. And how different that I-love-you had sounded.

I'd gone over it in my head so many times. It was the sort of thing you make your best friend talk about for hours and hours forever, except I couldn't because he was the only best friend I had. The only friend at all, really. We'd been at his house, sitting next to each other on his bed, watching part two of the ocean series. This one was about all the very crazy things down there, way at the bottom—creatures that were nothing but jagged gaping mouths, worms that could turn themselves inside out, fish that mated by dissolving their bodies into each other.

We were drinking that night, too, but only a little, and Xavier seemed drunker than it made sense for him to be. Our legs were touching on the bed and for some reason neither of us pulled away. Xavier leaned in close and picked up the locket I always wore—a little brass book that had been my grandmother's. It wasn't even really my style, but I never took it off because I loved her, and the locket was all of her that was left. He opened it and pretended to read. "Once there was a girl named Sasha who was the greeeatest in all the land," he said. Our faces were so close, I could feel his warm breath on my lips. He stayed there, holding the necklace, then looked up at me. He mumbled something and I had to ask him to repeat himself. "I love you so much" is what he said.

We said that sometimes as friends, so it's not like that was particularly weird or anything. But there was something about the way he was staring at me that was not the usual way at all. It made me feel so good, it wasn't even safe. Feeling that good could kill a person.

He let go of the necklace, then reached up like he was going to touch my face. I had wanted this for a very long time at that point. I had wanted it for so long and so badly that for just a second I let myself imagine it was actually happening in the real and normal way. But his eyes were all wrong, and I noticed then the prescription bottle on the windowsill. The top was off.

"I think you should get some rest," I said. He nodded and lay down. I flapped his blankets out over him, then sat on the

floor next to his bed. I poked him every couple minutes to make
sure he was only sleeping and not unconscious.

Those fucking pills.

Xavier's parents were good people, but they were also very
serious and uncomfortable with emotions and had no clue
what to do when Xavier's girlfriend dumped him and he basically stopped leaving his room. So they sent him to their regular family doctor, who whipped out a prescription pad.

"I know brain drugs can help people, and that's great. But
maybe you should see an actual shrink or something, too," is
what I said when he first told me about the doctor. "Like a
person who will, y'know, discuss some stuff?"

"Nope, don't need to," he'd said. "These will fix me right up."
He shook his pill bottles like maracas.

There were two kinds of pills: pink sticks to take "as needed"
that made Xavier loopy and forgetful, and little white oval
sleeping pills.

I'd put my hand on his shoulder, then made my voice all
dramatic, like I was in a cheesy TV movie. "There's not a pill for
a broken heart, Xavier," I'd said. Because sometimes pretending you're making is a joke is the only way to say the thing you
actually mean.

"Ah," said Xavier. He had half-smiled, which was the most
he smiled back then. "But apparently there is."

I sat with him, waking him up every few minutes, thinking about how if he'd meant that I-love-you in the way it had

sounded, it would change everything. How I *wanted* it to change everything.

But in the morning, Xavier had had no memory of the night before. The pills plus alcohol had switched his brain right off. He asked me what had happened. I told him he'd just seemed drunk, so I tucked him in and that was it.

Xavier hadn't been convinced. He asked me again and again, "Are you sure I didn't do anything terrible? Are you positive?"

"Well, if you really want to know, you can look at the video I put up on YouTube," I'd said finally. "We're getting soooooo many hits." And only then did he drop it.

After that he decided to stop taking the pills, to drink less. He started getting out of bed more. He went running once even. It was a turning point and he moved past it. I was happy for him. Relieved, obviously.

But still I couldn't stop thinking about that night. I wanted desperately to believe it had meant more than I knew it did. I googled "blackouts," looking for evidence that in a blacked-out state people reveal only the true truth of themselves. But I knew I wouldn't find any.

And I didn't.

The train sped on. We passed the bottle back and forth. By the time we got to our stop, it was half empty.

"Now be a normal person for a while," I said, playing our game.

"Don't ask me to do the impossible," said Xavier. He took my hand as we got off the train.

And I gave myself an instruction then, too: *Tell him by the end of the night. Tell him no matter what.*

I closed my eyes and breathed in, breathed out, and looked up at the moon. His hand was warm in mine, and the alcohol was warm in my belly.

I knew that night was going to change everything.

And it did, is the thing. It did.

Just not in ways I ever could have imagined.

Sasha

We walked toward the back of Sloe Joe's Tavern. Technically you were supposed to be twenty-one to go there at all, but nobody ever checked or cared.

It was hot and crowded and loud, like usual, with dim lights and red walls and a huge falling-apart crystal chandelier hanging over the dance floor. There was a rumor the chandelier was left over from when Sloe Joe's had been a speakeasy during Prohibition. There was another rumor that if you sat on the couch by the door, you'd catch crabs.

I loved everything about the place, especially the way all that sound drowned out all the thoughts in my head, rattled them around until I couldn't even think them, and then there was nothing but the heat and the stench of sweat and the feeling of music thumping inside me, beating in my chest like a heart.

It felt good to be back there with Xavier. This place used

to be *ours*. Back when we first became friends, we'd come here most weekends, back when weekends were ours, too.

Then he started dating Ivy and that changed. But I kept coming by myself after that. I liked going places alone. (Xavier was maybe the first and only person whose company I preferred to no one's.) I liked to be anonymous and watch people. I liked that when you were surrounded by people you didn't know, you could do and say whatever you wanted, and nothing counted.

I had a game, and the game was called Kiss a Stranger. The way you play is you look at a stranger and try to imagine what kissing them might be like.

And then you go and find out if you're right.

I liked the feeling of a mouth on my mouth. I liked that you could have an intense time with someone, crushed together in the dark, then let them go and never think about them again. Xavier said he was both baffled by and jealous of my ability to do that, because he was completely the opposite. "There are rocks inside the middle of you," he'd told me. He meant it as a compliment.

But in that moment with Xavier, I wasn't thinking about all of that. I was trying not to think of anything at all. There was a band onstage, a dozen people playing every instrument at once. And it was time to dance.

"Dance like no one's watching!!" I shouted at him, which was a joke we had about that corny saying you find on inspirational-quotes websites, superimposed over a picture of the ocean or whatever. Our joke was that it really meant dance while also picking peoples' pockets, because when no one is watching is the best time to be a thief. The game always progressed from there. *Dance like everyone's asleep! Dance like this room is full of ghosts! Dance like you just landed on Earth from space and what the hell is gravity even??!!*

But the thing was people *always* watched Xavier when he danced. It was something about the tallness, the broad shoulders, the sheer *size* of him, combined with the way he moved, rhythmic and graceful and lost in the moment entirely. In regular life he tried to make himself smaller, to take up less space, uncomfortable being a sweet introvert in the body of a big manly jock. But when he danced he seemed more sure of himself than he ever did in any other context. He seemed free.

Xavier bumped up against me and grinned that grin that he did when he was just a little bit drunk. The lights flashed. Xavier took the whisky from his bag.

Was it time to tell him? Even through all that alcohol the thought made my stomach twist. I wasn't ready. Not quite yet.

He cracked the top, took a sip. When he handed it to me, I gulped. The room shifted. We raised our arms and shook our hips. Another band went on. Cymbals and bells. More dancing.

Nsst nsst. Bzzz bzzz bzzz. We grinned wide white teeth glowing in the dark. The room was packed, people on all sides pushing us toward each other, arms and shoulders, knees colliding. What was I ever worried about? I smiled up at him. But when he looked down at me, he had this curious expression on his face, and maybe it was all the alcohol, but I swore he was staring at me in a very different way than usual. It was the same look I remembered from the night he'd forgotten.

I felt a delicate bubble of hope getting bigger and bigger inside my chest, terrifying and dangerous, but I could not even stop it.

Maybe this is happening, I told myself. *For real this time.*

A spotlight on stage lit up a singer all in glitter. She was enormous and gorgeous, like someone from another better planet. She leaned in toward the microphone. Her voice was a sex growl. "I wrote this song to be fucked to, but you could dance to it, too." She leaned back, and shouted, "WE ARE ALL GODDAMN MIRACLES!!" Music burst forth like confetti, the lights blinked on and off. I could feel Xavier's breath on my cheek.

And we were really dancing like no one was watching.

Closer.

Closer.

Closer.

But then I looked up and realized someone was.

She was over by the bar when the lights flashed, but I swear a second before I saw her, I'd felt her, deep in my gut the way some animals sense an earthquake just before it comes.

Holy fuck.

Ivy.

"Xavier," I said. The music was so loud. "XAVIER!" I grabbed his hand. He turned toward me, his mouth so close again. He was smiling, but I could barely see it, I could only smell the smell of him and feel his hard chest against my chest. Out of the corner of my eye, I saw motion near the bar. Ivy was making her way toward us.

My heart pounded and pounded. I felt like the building was on fire. Like the flames were about to swallow us whole. "Let's go outside!" I said.

Xavier nodded.

Then he froze.

"Oh God," he said. He'd seen her, too.

"C'mon!" I said. But he wasn't listening to me anymore.

Somehow she was always smaller than I remembered her. She was tiny and wiry in black knee-length cutoffs and an army-green tank top. She had a million metal bracelets on each wrist like armor and hair clumped and cut short, big eyes with eyeliner caked around them that had maybe been on for a couple of days. She had a pointed chin like a bat, a wide mouth, and a space between her two front teeth. The fact that Ivy wasn't convention-ally beautiful made it worse. Power you get from being beautiful is cheap. But Ivy's appeal just came from the *her* of her. She was a tornado, unpredictable and cracklingly alive. "She isn't scared of anything," Xavier had told me once with pride and awe. "Like literally not one single thing." *But* everyone *is scared of something* is what I had thought, though I didn't say it.

Ivy was right in front of us now. Xavier wasn't moving. Her friend Gwen was next to her. Gwen and I shared a nod. In elementary school Gwen and I had briefly been friends, good friends even. But that was a very long time ago.

The song ended, and the band started playing something else, slower and softer.

"I'm going to get another drink," Gwen said, then slipped away, as though maybe that had been the plan all along.

I stood there with Xavier and Ivy. The room swirled around us.

"It's been . . . ," Xavier said, finally. They hadn't been in contact at all since that day a month ago when everything happened.

"Too long," Ivy said. She pressed her flat hand against his chest. I stared at Ivy's short bitten nails and chipped silver polish. I imagined Ivy could feel Xavier's big sweet heart thumping against her palm. "I need to talk to you," Ivy said. I saw Ivy glance at my blue hands, then up at Xavier's hair. "Give us a minute?" she said to me.

I turned toward Xavier. I knew I needed to stop this, whatever was about to happen. But when our eyes met, I realized it was already too late. "I'll find you soon?" he said.

I froze, as everything I wasn't saying bubbled up inside me. Ivy was a monster and would destroy him. And last time he just barely survived her. And this was supposed to be the night I finally told him the truth. I had waited so long for this.

"Sash?" Xavier said. He sounded so gentle and concerned. "Is that okay?"

Later I would think back to this moment, wonder if

everything might have been different if only I'd given a different answer.

"Okay," I said. "Sure."

I turned away, then pushed through the crowd. When I looked back, Xavier and Ivy had been swallowed up.

I got in line for the bathroom. I was a wild and desperate animal. I needed to do something, to stop this, to save him. But I had no idea what.

Gwen walked by holding a drink. She gulped it down and put the empty glass on a table. She gave me a little wave as she headed toward the front door. I called out to her. "Gwen! Wait!"

Gwen came back. "Where are you going?" I said.

"Home," Gwen said. She looked at my hands. "So . . . is that like a weird fetish thing or something?" She grinned.

I remembered when we were friends back in fourth grade, going over to her house. It was fancy and completely silent. Gwen lived there with her father, who was always at work, and her mother, who spent all day in bed. Gwen had said that this was because her mother was very popular and had a lot of friends who lived far away in other countries in other time zones and she stayed up very late at night talking to them. "That's why she's in bed," Gwen said. "During the day she has to catch up on sleep. Also sometimes at night she goes to parties." The story had seemed kind of strange to me at the time, but I had reminded myself my own mother did plenty of weird things. Who could really say why mothers did what they did?

Gwen's mother passed away a few years after that. We weren't friends anymore by that point, but I'd heard that she had been sick for a long time, had spent years slowly dying. I understood then what the story had been about. The idea of my once friend inviting people over and then telling that lie to cover up what was actually happening made my chest hurt. I went to the funeral alone and sat at the back. I'm not sure if Gwen even saw me.

Standing there that night at Sloe Joe's, I thought of Gwen's silent house, her sick mother, of how easy it is to lose someone and how there are so many different ways for it to happen.

"She came here looking for him, you know," Gwen said.

"She did?" That made it worse. But I wondered why Gwen was telling me this. "How did she even know he'd be here?"

Gwen shrugged. "She just figured, I guess. Haven't you noticed how good she is at that?"

"At what?" I said.

"Getting what she wants." Gwen gave me a half smile. "Have a good night, girly." She turned and headed toward the door again.

I stayed in line, breathing hard.

If Ivy bumping into him here wasn't an accident, it meant she wanted something from him. Maybe she even wanted him back.

But that doesn't mean she can have him, I reminded myself.

I imagined leaving the bathroom and finding him. He would be alone. "So where'd you know that girl from?" he'd say. "She looked familiar, but I couldn't place her. What was her name? Plant? Root?" And he'd grin, at his own dumb joke.

And he'd take the whisky out of his bag.

And we'd go outside and finish it.

And we'd play our game again.

And finally, finally, I would tell him the truth.

Only when I got back from the bathroom, he was nowhere to be found. He wasn't on the dance floor, wasn't at the bar. Finally, I headed out to the tiny concrete courtyard in the back where people went to smoke sometimes. There was a group sitting around a picnic table, passing a vaporizer. I turned toward the corner, and that's when I spotted them. Xavier and Ivy, up against the wall, their eyes were closed. They weren't kissing or moving or anything, they were just like that, holding each other tight.

I felt hot and sick, full of rage and terror.

I backed up quickly, before they saw me. I went through the bar, outside into the hot night, and then I was gone.

My heart pounded powerfully, painfully. I didn't know then what I know now: Be careful when your feelings are too strong, when you love someone too much. A heart too full is like a bomb. One day it will explode.

Xavier

They say guys make stupid decisions with their dicks, but Xavier knew the very dumbest ones he'd ever made were the ones he made with his heart.

Ivy held his hand as she led him through the trees toward that place in the woods, midway between their houses, where they always used to go. She squeezed tight like she was trying to keep him from running away. He probably should have run—some part of him knew that—but his stupid heart kept marching him forward.

When he'd seen Ivy at Sloe Joe's, he'd tried to remind himself that he was supposed to be mad, but all he'd felt was surprised, and maybe a little bit scared, and mostly just very, very happy to see her.

She brought him outside to the courtyard, and instead of saying anything, she'd just wrapped her arms around him and stayed like that. And then after a while asked him, please would he please come with her to their spot in the woods, and he said okay.

On the train, she'd leaned her head back against his chest and nestled into him like the whole last month of them being apart hadn't even happened. When he caught sight of them together in the reflection in the glass, he saw that he was smiling.

Now they walked in between the trees where there was no path, but they both knew the way blackout drunk with their eyes closed. They'd come here together so many times, starting back when it was still winter but the smell of spring was creeping in over the melting snow. "It's the time of year to fuck against a tree in the woods" is what Ivy had told him when she'd brought him the first time. And then she'd taken off his gloves and put his hands up under her coat and sweater onto her warm skin.

Now, the air was hot and thick in that late-July way. And as he followed her, he tried not to think about the last time they'd spoken before this. He tried not to think about how he'd gone to a party in a neighboring town to hear his friend Ethan's band play on a night Ivy had said she was busy with a family thing. But then he found her there, out back next to one of the kegs, wrapped up in a skinny punk-looking guy with a septum ring and a leather cuff on each wrist. And when she looked up and saw him seeing her, she didn't even seem surprised. Almost like she'd expected to get caught, or wanted to. "Oh shit, is this the chump you've been texting me about?" the punk guy asked. And he laughed.

Xavier tried not to think about how he'd waited to hear from her after that, assumed she'd come to him full of apologies, like she usually did after she'd done something messed up, only this time she didn't. And he tried not to think about how a week after that he'd gone back to their place in the woods, because it was late and he couldn't sleep and maybe some part of him hoped she might be out there missing him like he'd been missing her. And the crazy thing is, she *was* there. But she wasn't alone. Turned out, she didn't think of it as her and Xavier's spot the way he did. He left as quickly as he could. They never heard Xavier running in those woods. They were making too much noise on their own.

He was trying not to think about that then as Ivy pulled him forward, twigs cracking under their feet. The moon was so bright, everything was glowing. The farther away from the rest of the world they went, the easier it was to tell himself that all of this was happening outside of regular space and time and didn't count. That he could have this one night, whatever this was, and not even have to pay for it later.

Now they had reached the place where they always used to go, but there was something new: a tire dangling from a tree branch, connected to a rope that did not look thick or strong enough to hold it. Ivy pressed a button on the swing and a string of lights glowed yellow.

Ivy leaped up onto the swing, stuck one leg out behind her. She had taken ballet for years as a kid and could still move like that, like the air that surrounded her was different than regular air, thicker and thinner both. And when she smiled at him, everything else was wiped away, and the only thing in his mind and his heart was how very much he had missed her.

She lowered herself down, slipped both legs into the middle of the tire. "Wind me up, please," she said, like a kid asking him to play. Ivy was so many things all at once. And so he held her hand and walked circles around her until the rope was high and tight and it seemed like it might snap. And then he let her go and she spun and spun as the rope unwound. She leaned her head back, and she opened her mouth like she was screaming, but no sound came out. When the spinning stopped, she got off the swing and pulled him to her.

That's when he realized she was crying.

"I am such a shit," she said. "I'm an absolute horrible, awful shithead."

His heart was beating so hard. "Wait," he said. All he wanted then was for her to stop crying. When Ivy cried, it felt like the only thing in the world that mattered. "Please . . ." But as he searched for the right words, she raised her hand to his lips to quiet him, shook her head, and looked down.

"I deserve for you to hate me." She looked up at him, blinked her big wet eyes. "Do you?"

And he told her what he'd always told her when she cried

over something she'd done—that everyone makes mistakes. And of course he didn't hate her. He never could.

She stood on her tiptoes and leaned in close.

Xavier had heard that the moment before an accident time slows down. One second feels like a minute, an hour, a month. That's what it was like then, out there in those woods, her lips inching toward his so slowly, his heart racing, stomach twisting, like he knew this kiss would either kill him or save him.

"This is a terrible idea," he said quietly, right before their lips touched. "This is definitely going to end in disaster."

"Not this time," she said. "I promise this time. Nothing bad will happen."

Later he would look back at that night and remember how they'd both believed so much in the truth of what they'd said.

It's just that only one of them was right.

Sasha

I stood at the station, waiting for the train, staring into the dark empty tracks, trying not to picture the things I could not stop picturing. Xavier and Ivy out in the courtyard, pressed together. Xavier and Ivy kissing. Xavier and Ivy, wherever they were now, her hand against his chest, reaching in, tearing out his heart, putting it into her mouth, and eating it.

Somehow I ended up with the rest of the whisky. I was sick and hollow and needed this to stop, so I sipped and sipped until it was gone. But it didn't fix anything.

I closed my eyes and new images filled my head, ones that hurt as much as the others, maybe more: Xavier's face so close to mine, his grin seeming to mean something I so desperately wanted it to.

It hadn't always been painful with me and Xavier. There was

a whole year before this when we were friends and only friends. *Best* friends. And that was it.

We were in the same English class and paired up for a project. I had assumed Xavier was just this regular guy, boring and normal. But the more I got to know him, the more I realized I'd been unfair. He was smart. And weird and silly. And so talented. One day I was eating Swedish Fish and I gave him one, and he stuck it to his notebook and drew an entire little world around it, strange and funny and beautiful. Another time he spent the entire class passing me a series of notes, each containing only a single letter, spelling out *THIS IS A VERY INEFFICENT WAY TO WRITE A NOTE*. Another day he brought in a hollowed-out penny and showed me a magic trick he'd learned on YouTube. "My backup career idea is amateur street magician," he'd said. "What's your non-backup career idea?" I'd asked. "Sorcerer," he'd said.

Eventually I got to know him well enough to realize this: he delighted in the small things, but also knew that in the grand scheme of the world, nothing we did or felt mattered at all. And he got how that was unbelievably terrifying, but also was the thing that made us free.

But even though nothing mattered and a person could basically do whatever they wanted, he was still kind. Not just nice, but truly *kind*, which is different.

He never judged anyone for anything or about anything. He was boundlessly forgiving. He was sensitive and didn't know how to protect himself sometimes. He said I had an unshakable core and he envied me. "Being in love is a painful nightmare," he'd told me once. "You're lucky because your heart is too tough for it." He thought it was true. So had I.

But he is how I learned I was wrong.

I remembered what he'd told me when we were first becoming friends. We were at his house working on our English project, talking about dating people, and I told him how I didn't really believe in it. "Make out and move on," I said. "That's my MO." I did a corny grin.

He had told me he had a history of getting crushes on girls who always thought he was too normal to bother with at first (just like I had, though of course I never told him)— tough weirdos, girls who played drums, who pierced their own ears, who made robots in their basements, girls who wore shit-kicking boots and actually used them to kick shit. Girls who maybe he liked more than they liked him, who he never quite had even when he had them. And who always ended up breaking his heart.

"I guess maybe my MO is mmmmm optimistic," he said. "Because every time, I always have lots of hope and think it's gonna turn out great. Or maybe Moron, Obviously. Because . . . obviously."

I remembered when he first told me the whole thing, I'd thought the girls he described sounded maybe a little similar to me. And I'd really hoped he would never like me as anything more than a friend—I would've hated to have to hurt his big sweet heart. He was not my type at all. The guys I usually liked were androgynous and pretty. And besides, I'd had no interest in dating anyone, anyway.

Back then I couldn't have imagined what would happen later, how everything would twist around inside me. But that's the thing about life. No matter how smart you are, you'll just never be able to imagine any of what's coming for you, not until it's right there, standing on your throat.

It was after 2:30 in the morning when I finally got home, but the moment I walked into my room, the bone-deep exhaustion that promised to take me swiftly to sleep burned away. And there I was, alone, wide-awake, and drunk.

I took out my phone and texted Xavier. Hope you're ok wherever you are . . . I held my breath, waited for the texting dots, just in case. I imagined what he might write back: You won't believe the ridiculous night I had . . . or maybe Is it too early for birthday diner breakfast? I stared at my phone. But no message appeared.

What could he be doing at that moment? I didn't want to imagine. But I couldn't help it. Maybe he and Ivy were still at Sloe Joe's. Maybe they were dancing slowly in the corner out of time to the music. Maybe they were having full-on sex out back in the courtyard. People did that sometimes, I had seen them.

STOP!

I tried to remind myself that I would talk to Xavier tomorrow, and there was nothing I could *do* now. But I also knew that when a story grabs ahold of you, it won't let you go until it's ready.

Maybe they were on the train together. Maybe Ivy was falling asleep on him and he was gazing lovingly at the top of her head. Maybe they were at that spot in the woods, maybe she was sneaking Xavier into her house.

Maybe.

Maybe.

Maybe.

All of a sudden, something occurred to me: If I really needed to know what was going on, I didn't have to torture myself imagining. I could torture myself with real, actual information if I just checked Ivy's Instagram.

Ivy's awful Instagram.

Back at the very beginning when they first got together, Xavier checked it constantly. He'd get a hit of the Ivy drug every time she put up something new, which was multiple times a day. "She has a ton of random dude followers who comment on her pictures and stuff," Xavier had said. "They are big users of that tongue emoji. They are always posting the tongue to her. But it doesn't actually matter." Xavier had told me that Ivy said she'd let any guy follow her so long as his avatar pic was of a real human being and he didn't seem to be a bot. He'd said she thought it was funny to have all these random creeps commenting. When Xavier told me all of this, it sort of sounded like he was trying to convince himself, like he didn't quite believe it was all so harmless, but really, really wanted to.

After they broke up, Xavier couldn't stop looking. "Please help me," he'd said. "Throw my phone out the window or remove my eyeballs or something." He held up his phone. There was a supersaturated picture of Ivy in the foreground of the screen, a wiry male arm draped over her shoulder, a leather cuff wrapped around the guy's wrist. Xavier squished his eyes shut and turned his head away while I clicked unfollow.

But now, I went to her page. Ivy was on there under the name Twisted Tree, username TwistedTree16. The avatar photo was a close-up of a mouth with the tongue out and nothing more, so if you didn't already know it was her, you'd never be able to figure it out. And the account was locked.

Of course it was.

Xavier said her parents were super nosy and tried to monitor everything she did ever since they caught her drinking with an older boy when she was thirteen. She had to make sure to log out of her computer every time she left the house so they couldn't snoop through her email, and never leave her phone unguarded even for a second. "They've threatened to kick her out if they catch her doing one more 'bad' thing," Xavier had said, back when he and Ivy had first started hanging out. "I think they're this close to actually doing it."

I stared at the mouth and the little closed padlock. I felt

then a strange mix of disappointment and relief. I wanted to see what was in there, but also oh so desperately did not.

But this wasn't about me. This was about Xavier. This was about the dark black pit he was finally, finally almost out of. This was about all the damage Ivy could do—*would* do—if I didn't gather enough information to keep it from happening somehow.

At least that's what I told myself.

I knew I should have stopped then. I knew I should have let it go, gone to bed, dealt with it in the morning.

But I didn't. I couldn't.

Because my beast of a brain already had a plan.

Xavier

Xavier and Ivy stared at each other googly-eyed, kiss-drunk. "I really missed you," she said. And then she held his face in her hands and looked right at him in this way that overwhelmed him with love. During moments like this, it was impossible to remember the bad things that had happened. This feeling was the real one. Everything else was just noise.

"I can't believe I ever let you go," Ivy said. "There is no one as kind or as sweet as you. Like literally no one on earth. I am garbage."

"You're not," Xavier said. "Stop saying . . ."

But then Ivy did something, something he would think about later, something he would replay in his head over and over so many times, trying to understand it.

She took both his hands, brought them up to her face,

held one on each cheek and looked him straight in the eye. Then she lowered his hands down to her collar.

"Do it," she said.

Xavier didn't understand. "Do what?"

"Choke me." She tried to wrap his hands around her neck. She tried to get him to squeeze. It took a while for his brain to process what was even happening. He started to pull away. She wouldn't let him.

"No. I don't want to."

"But I deserve it," she said. "And you *do* want to. I can tell."

Xavier realized then that they were both drunker than he'd thought. And that he really, really, did not like the feeling of his hands around her throat. He did not like how thin her neck felt, how easy it would be to break her.

"No," he said. "Stop! I don't want that at all!"

He tried to pull away again. This time she let him go.

"Just kidding," she said. Then she buried her face in his chest. "You still smell the same. It's very hard to remember a smell, but I swear I always could with you. . . ."

And then she kissed him again, harder this time. She kissed him and wiped every thought he'd ever had out of his brain. She kissed him and pressed up against him, and when she reached into the hole in the tree for the big box of condoms she'd put there in the spring and there was only one left in the box, he tried not to think about what had happened to the others.

Xavier wondered if later he would regret this. He wondered if later he'd remember this moment and wish he could go back and drag himself out of the woods and stop whatever happened next. The problem with time is it only ever goes forward. And when you are careening toward disaster, you never know it until it is way too late.

Sasha

I knew what I was doing was fucked up, but if I was going to do it, I was going to do it right. I picked a name too common for easy googling (Jake Jones) and a location (a random town about thirty miles away) and wrote an innocuous bio line ("Some random guy"). I told myself my intentions were pure—I just wanted to see how much danger Xavier was in exactly. So I could figure out how to save him. If some part of me already had other more elaborate plans, well, at least I wasn't aware of it.

I made up a new Jake Jones email address and an Instagram account to link it to, then got some fake followers by signing up for a free trial of some shady music streaming service.

I followed a bunch of accounts to make my following and followers numbers look normal. I uploaded a bunch of close-ups of the white wall of my bedroom, to give myself a reasonable number of posts. I was going to set the account to private anyway, so it's not like Ivy would be able to see what my pictures were, she just needed to see that I had some, that I was real.

Now all I needed was a photo of a guy. One that didn't appear online anywhere so it wasn't reverse image searchable. A guy of about the right age, good-looking but not unbelievably so.

I went upstairs to my bedroom closet, dug around in the back until I found the little digital camera I'd had five summers ago when I got sent to a sleepaway camp that didn't allow phones while my mom was dating a chef who hated kids. I got the charger, plugged in the camera, flipped it on, and found the perfect picture of a dude in his late teens with dark hair that stuck up in the front, a big pouty, almost feminine, mouth, and a swim-instructor body, which made sense because he was one.

I uploaded the photo, then cropped it so you could see only half the face, half a tongue, and one muscular bicep, and hit save. And then, just like that, Jake was real. My eyes were closing. It was almost four. So I did the thing this was all leading up to: I went to Ivy's page again, and I clicked "request to follow."

I took a deep breath. I stood up. The room shifted and I remembered how drunk I still was. I told myself that if I regretted it in the morning, I could just delete the account. I'd delete the account and no one would ever know, and it would be like none of this ever happened.

I got into bed then, and, too exhausted to torture me anymore, my brain was quiet. And finally I went to sleep.

Xavier

"**Come to my house. I** promise we won't get caught," she said. "I promise, I promise, I promise, I promise, I promise, I promise, I promise." She said it until the word "promise" was nothing but mouth sounds and Xavier was laughing.

"We'll have to be very quiet once we get inside," she said. "Until tomorrow morning when my parents go to the marriage counselor they think I don't know they go to. Good thing you already made me scream."

Tomorrow this will be done, he told himself. Tomorrow he would do the smart thing and cut this off, if she hadn't already. He'd just let himself have one night of this, and then be finished again. For good this time.

That's what he told himself. But even then, he knew he was lying.

Sasha

I woke up to my mother standing in my bedroom door, a pair of Minnie Mouse ears on top of her head. "We're back and we brought you a lil' present, sleepyhead," she said, all charming and folksy, as though that was actually the way she talked to me. Which I guessed she did now, ever since Marc came around. She took the ears off her head and tossed them onto the bed.

If I have any natural skills as a liar, she's how I got them. With every new boyfriend, my mom "reinvented herself," which is what she would have called all the lying if anyone ever confronted her about it, which no one would have, because I was the only one who knew. I saw the way my mother twisted herself around, as though the facts of one's past and one's personality could be slipped into and out of like a coat. I saw how easy it was to make fake things seem real.

I sat up in bed. "Aw thanks!" I said, loud and cheery. "Welcome home!" I always played along. It was easier that way. "You girls sure do have fun" is what Marc had said once. Girls, both of us.

They'd been together a year and a half now, my mom and Marc. She met him around the time I met Xavier. The version of herself she was with him was very different than the one she'd been with the last two guys. With Edwin she'd been aloof and frosty, and for a brief period had suggested I call her "Caroline" instead of "Mom." With Richard she'd taken an interest in my schoolwork and kept trying to cook for me, which I actually didn't mind because she's good at it. But it only lasted three weeks. With Marc mom was boisterous and friendly, as much as she could be, and almost never around. Which was how I liked it.

My mom was better with a boyfriend. I guess that sounds sad, but it was also just true. On her own she was restless and angry. She thought everything in the whole world was bad and everyone was bad, and everywhere she looked she found evidence to support this. It got worse after her mother, my grandma, the one whose locket I wore, died two years before, even though I knew my mother hadn't really liked her. My grandmother had gotten terrible dementia the year prior, and my mother was the one who found the nursing home, the one who made sure Grandma was getting good care. She'd been the only one of her siblings to visit regularly. I knew she resented it, but she also seemed to secretly like it, too, because it confirmed her belief about how selfish they were. My mother likes to be right, even about bad things. Maybe about bad things especially.

Marc is twenty-three years older than my mother and the owner of a large chain of budget two-star hotels in popular vacation destinations. He spent all his time traveling between them, checking their quality. Since they'd gotten together, he took my mother along with him.

She actually seemed kind of happy. And I was glad for her. I was also glad when she was gone. He left stacks of cash for me "for food and stuff" when they went out of town, but it was always way too much, like two hundred dollars for a three-day trip when there were already groceries in the fridge. At first I tried to refuse it—it felt weird taking his money like that. But it made my mother upset when I didn't. "Sasha, stop it. Marc will feel bad," she said once, when I deposited the pile of twenties back on the kitchen table. As if keeping Marc happy was our shared goal. So I kept it after that, never spent it, let it build up in a pile in the bottom drawer of my dresser.

"Come down and say hi," my mother said. And I nodded. When she shut the door my phone buzzed. A text from Xavier.

HAPPY BIRTHDAY PAL!! he wrote. He was doing the joke we always did.

Thank you, so kind of you to remember, I wrote back. I was definitely born, there's no doubt about that

Funny that you were ever a baby, he wrote, you are waaaaaaay bigger now

There was a pause then. Dots appeared. Stopped. Came back.

I know how sorry you are for going off last night, so don't worry. . . . I forgive you he wrote. I wondered what he (as me) was forgiving himself for. Just the stuff with Ivy? The moment before? The almost kiss?

Thank you You're a true pal I wrote.

You are too he wrote back.

So . . . what happened with Ivy? I wrote. I was breaking the joke. I hated having to ask.

There was a pause then, texting dots appeared and disappeared and reappeared and disappeared again. My heart pounded. I wondered how many heart attacks each year are caused by those little hell dots. Finally a message:

Will tell you later. Don't worry, everythings good ☺

What did that mean?

It was then that I remembered what I'd done the night before, the person I'd created.

I went to Instagram to see if "Jake" had been granted access. He had.

Suddenly Ivy's feed was right in front of me, hundreds of perfect little squares in full-saturated color. The most recent picture was of Ivy and Gwen from the night before, faces pressed together, WINESTAINSMILE was the caption. There was nothing new of Xavier. Maybe "everythings good" really did mean that he was being smart this time. They had a drunken hug, shared a nostalgic moment. Maybe they'd talked, she'd apologized, and then that was it.

But there were so many more pictures, so much more to look at. I knew I shouldn't, but somehow I couldn't stop myself.

There were a few photos of her wearing ballet shoes with regular clothes, doing crazy ballet poses in everyday situations, one of her in full makeup, devouring a meatball sub, a close-up of a Popsicle-stained tongue, a looped video of her rolling back and forth on a pair of roller skates, a few pictures of a very fluffy dog.

I scrolled back a few months, looked at the ones from right around New Year's. There was a shot of a guy from far away. He was running up a hill in the snow in a T-shirt and shorts, the slanty winter sun setting behind him, surrounding him with light. This was Xavier from the first time the two of them had met.

Xavier had told me the story, and I'd thought about it so many times, I felt like I had been there myself.

He had been out running on a Sunday afternoon, the last day of winter break—he loved to run in the winter, outside in the freezing cold with nothing in his ears but the wind. They lived not too far from each other, Xavier and Ivy, though he hadn't known that at the time. He was running by her house and she was standing at the end of her driveway, while he made his way up the hill, just standing there watching him. When he got close, she'd yelled, "Hey, I'll be your alibi if you want." He stopped, confused, asked her what she meant. "For whatever crime you're fleeing the scene of," she said. "That's the only reason a person would be out running in this. If anyone asks what you were doing, I'll tell them we were fucking." And she stared at him and didn't even crack a smile. Then invited him to come inside her house. He said the whole thing had been so strange and confusing he didn't know what to do but say yes. And that's how it started.

Just then a new picture appeared in Ivy's feed. There was a face out of focus in the background, a shock of blue hair behind one ear, mouth half open, smiling, eyes closed. In the front of the frame was a spoonful of vanilla ice cream with Froot Loops stuck into it. This had been Xavier's favorite special-occasion treat as a kid. He had asked for it every birthday growing up. It became a tradition for him even after his parents stopped doing it.

Last year, I was the one who got it for him.

Xavier

The morning of his seventeenth birthday, the first thing Xavier felt was a body sliding up against him, and then a kiss on the cheek, and hot breath near his ear. "Eyes closed, mouth open," Ivy said.

Then she fed him something. Xavier was smiling before he even swallowed.

She remembered.

He felt her get up off the bed. He opened his eyes. She was across the room, back to him, walking to the bathroom. The summer sun was coming through the window and her sheer curtains. She was naked and unselfconscious in a way he couldn't imagine ever being. It didn't feel safe to look at her. It didn't feel safe because of what it did to him.

Don't let this happen again, Xavier told himself. He couldn't believe he was there. He thought about the night before, after all the stuff in the woods, Ivy convincing him to come stay over. She promised they wouldn't get caught, as though that was the only thing to be concerned about.

"That's maybe not the best idea . . . ," Xavier had said.

"But the maybe-not-the-best ideas *are* the best ideas, aren't they?" Ivy had smiled that smile that meant she knew there was no way Xavier could resist her.

And she had been right.

Xavier had texted his mom that he was staying at Sasha's. His parents trusted him so much that it would never even occur to them that Xavier could lie. Which made him feel especially guilty when he did.

Xavier stared at Ivy's back, then forced himself to look away. He reached for his jeans on the floor, took his phone out of the pocket, and for a moment Xavier was back in the real world. He saw the text from Sasha sent late the night before.

Sasha.

Xavier thought again about the great birthday time they'd been having. It was the first real fun Xavier had had in so long. And he thought of how for a moment it had seemed like . . . well, Xavier didn't know exactly. It seemed like the air between them had shifted or something. Like things were inching in a strange direction. Xavier wasn't even sure if he had been making it up or not. And then Ivy appeared.

But here, in Ivy's room on the morning of his seventeenth birthday, he felt certain he'd imagined all that Sasha stuff.

Which Xavier knew was a good thing, for a bunch of different reasons, not least of which was the fact that Sasha was his best friend on earth.

Now in the bright light of day, he felt weird that he'd left Sasha and gone off with Ivy. Not that Sasha would care about the being alone part—she *liked* to be alone—but because she might care about who he'd gone off with.

He found himself defending his decision to Sasha in his head. Defending Ivy. She wasn't all good or all bad. She was human and complicated and confusing, like all of us. True, she made messes sometimes. But she never meant to and she always felt awful about it after. And Xavier didn't quite understand her, but then again, could you ever really understand anyone? He didn't understand Sasha, either. Sasha, who was always so strong. Who only ever did what was right. She was solid and secure and never needed anyone. But Xavier wasn't like that.

And besides, Sasha hadn't heard Ivy apologizing in the woods, and hadn't seen the look on Ivy's face this morning when she'd kissed him. Ivy had done some not-so-great stuff, but Xavier didn't blame her, and maybe it was dumb and naive not to, but he just didn't. Life messes us up in so many ways, messes all of us right the hell up. And when we fumble and bumble around, crashing into one another, stepping on toes and hearts, it's not on purpose. Being a person is nearly impossible.

He heard the toilet flush and Ivy's bare feet padding across the shiny wood floors. And then she was back in the room and Xavier forgot everything else. She stood by the door, watching him, one arm raised up against the frame, dark hair sticking straight up.

Xavier started to get out of bed. She sprang forward and then her hands were over his eyes and her mouth was against his ear again.

"Not yet," she said.

For the next hour, Xavier was just a body. Lips. Hands. Skin. A beating heart. And when they were done, they were wrapped together in her sheets, and Xavier was full of all the chemicals, those love ones or the post-sex ones that are impossible to distinguish between. She grabbed her hairbrush, which she hardly ever used herself, and started pulling it through his hair with long, smooth strokes. She did this all the time when they were dating. "You're like the doll I always wanted as a kid," she had said once. Xavier took it as a compliment at first. He was the thing she'd always wanted. After they broke up, Xavier told Sasha the story and she had raised one eyebrow in that wary way she didn't know she did. "It's kind of fucked she said that to you," Sasha said. "As though you are just a *thing*." *That's not how she meant it*, Xavier had wanted to tell her. He wanted Sasha to understand, but he was so tired back then, he could barely speak at all.

Now, that morning in Ivy's bed, Xavier was trying not to

think of anything at all as she brushed and brushed. But then Ivy's phone vibrated, and she reached for it, and the corner of her mouth twitched up into a special kind of smirk. His stomach was immediately tight. Xavier *knew* that smirk. But Xavier also knew it was ridiculous to be jealous. He and Ivy weren't actually together. They weren't going to be. This was just for today.

But Xavier was wrong about the smirk and what it was, because she turned her phone toward him. On the screen was a guy's Instagram account, locked. The guy was maybe a couple of years older than they were, though it was hard to say, because the picture was cropped so you could only really see half of him, half a handsome face, one muscular arm.

"Look," she said. "An arm followed me." She stuck her tongue through her teeth, then tossed her phone onto the nightstand. She slid close to him. A second later her phone buzzed again. This time, after she looked at it, she frowned and pulled away.

"My parents are on their way back. You have to go now." Her tone was totally different then, all business. It was something he'd almost let himself forget about her, how quickly she flipped from one thing to another. "This was fun. It was good to see you."

Xavier stood, gathered up his T-shirt, jeans, the one sock he wasn't wearing. Adrenaline was coursing through him. *This was fun. It was good to see you.* Those were ending words—those were the words of this being done again. *Of course*, he told himself. That was the plan all along, one night and that's it. He knew it was for the best, but in that moment it really, really did not feel that way.

Suddenly, Xavier was filled with dread at the idea of going home with this finished again, returning to the hard work of getting over her, made all the harder now that Xavier remembered so clearly what being with her was like. Because what is getting over someone if not a slow, excruciating forgetting? Ivy was very, very hard to forget.

He started getting dressed, putting his clothes on in reverse of the order Ivy had taken them off him—underwear, T-shirt, jeans. Xavier imagined himself in a video playing backward, the love Xavier poured out at her being funneled back into his chest, the taste of her lips leaving his, walking backward out of that room, shutting closed his heart.

He walked toward the door. He turned to wave.

"Wait," Ivy said. "You forgot something." She ran toward him, then jumped up, wrapped her legs around his waist. "This isn't over," she whispered. "I won't fuck it up this time. I mean it."

Sasha

A good girl would have played it different.

Good Girls do not scheme or plot. Good Girls do not twist and sneak. When their best friend calls them on his birthday and says in this shy, squirrelly, embarrassed way, *I know this is going to sound stupid, but I think we're kind of seeing each other again, maybe,* Good Girls say, *Xavier, listen* and *Xavier, I'm concerned.* And when their best friend says, *We're going to take things slow, and I promise to be careful,* but they can hear in his voice that he is already long gone and is only trying his best to sound reasonable, but he is far past reasonable, like someone who has newly been recruited into a cult, Good Girls calmly say their piece, and step back, as he does not listen, does not listen, does not listen, and makes the same mistakes, only worse this time. Good Girls tell themselves, *Well, I tried my best and it is not up to me and you have to let people make their own choices,* and then they watch as his once-ex-now-current-girlfriend wraps herself around his neck and chokes him until he's dead.

But Bad Girls know it's never that simple.

Bad Girls know everything is gray. Everything is messy and complicated. And sometimes you have to do some fucked-up stuff to make things okay.

Bad Girls sink their teeth in.

Bad Girls use every weapon they have.

Bad Girls know there is no right and no wrong. There is just what you're willing to do. What you *need* to do.

Here is what I did.

July 21, 11:24 p.m.

JakeJones1717: Well, having scrolled through your Instagram photos, I've come to the conclusion that if there's an infinite number of parallel worlds, there's at least one in which you and I are already best friends

JakeJones1717: oops, sorry. That was a typo

JakeJones1717: I meant fucking

July 21, 11:35 p.m.

TwistedTree16: In how many of the infinite worlds do you think I just punched you in the balls?

JakeJones1717: 92300329 where I deserved it. 3 where I didn't

TwistedTree16: TWO WHERE YOU DIDN'T

JakeJones1717: Fair

TwistedTree16: But in those 2 you probably liked it, I can tell your type. Perv

JakeJones1717: Okay, but seriously I'm not actually a creepy perv. Just messing around on here and I guess if we're being totally honest, looking for cute girls to talk to because everyone I know in actual life is boring as hell

JakeJones1717: I like your pics, your dog is really fluffy. What's her name?

TwistedTree16: Dog talk is boring. Maybe YOURE as boring as the people you know. I liked perv you better

JakeJones1717: If you want perv, I can do perv

TwistedTree16: I just said I liked it BETTER than boring dog talk

JakeJones1717: Okay fair. What do YOU want to talk about?

TwistedTree16: You wrote me first. I might not want to talk about anything

JakeJones1717: But you're answering me aren't you . . .

TwistedTree16: Maybe I'M just bored

JakeJones1717: Okay, good point. In another one of those worlds we are having this exact conversation, but it's going better

JakeJones1717: Can we try again?

TwistedTree16: If there's an infinite number of parallel worlds, there's one in which you and I are already fucking

TwistedTree16: oops, sorry. That was a typo

TwistedTree16: I meant "dead"

JakeJones1717: I think you probably meant *in love*

July 22, 10:13 a.m.

JakeJones1717: In how many of the parallel worlds am I as hungover as I am in this one, do you think? Serious question

TwistedTree16: Maybe like 4

JakeJones1717: Oh god . . . that's not many if we're talking about infinity. Though it is impossible to imagine anyone more hungover than I am right now . . . so maybe 4 is good?

TwistedTree16: If it makes you feel any better, in like 6 you just died of alcohol poisoning

JakeJones1717: Dark. At least those other Jakes are out of their misery

TwistedTree16: Parallel worlds are no kinder than this one

JakeJones1717: I'm going to go try and flush my own head down the toilet now

TwistedTree16: Are you trying to talk dirty to me?

TwistedTree16: but really . . . let me know how it goes. Most people who show up in my DMs are dumb boring idiots. You seem fun

JakeJones1717: Awww, are you flirting with me, Twisted?

TwistedTree16: Well I'm not NOT not not NOT NOT not not flirting with you. If you see what I'm saying

JakeJones1717: oh god. That is really confusing

JakeJones1717: hey . . . so I don't mean to be presumptuous or anything, but can I have your number? Maybe I'll text you sometime . . . and when I do I WILL be flirting

TwistedTree16: _ _ _ - _ _ _ - _ _ _ _

JakeJones1717: what's that?

TwistedTree16: have you ever played hangman?

JakeJones1717: Yeah . . .

TwistedTree16: that's hangman for my phone number, if you guess it, you can text me . . .

JakeJones1717: Are there any A's?

TwistedTree16: it's a phone NUMBER?

JakeJones1717: I stand by my question . . .

JakeJones1717: *s??

TwistedTree16: oh my god. Okay. 914-555-7278. That either IS or IS NOT my phone number. Text it and find out

Xavier

Xavier went back home late in the morning of his seventeenth birthday, still smelling like Ivy. He was hungover and had barely slept, but somehow he was wide-awake.

And he had no idea what to think or how to feel.

Back in his room, outside of the bubble of the woods, of Ivy's house and bed, everything from the night before felt like it had happened to someone else a very long time ago.

He knew he should call Sasha then. But the idea of trying to explain it all, of somehow trying to justify this . . .

He remembered when they had first become friends. They were in the same English elective but they'd never really talked before. Xavier could tell she was smart from the things she'd say in class. And he could tell she was tough because she didn't ever look nervous when called on, and because she was always alone in the halls but did not seem to mind it. He liked the necklaces she wore—a little metal book that she was often fiddling with, and sometimes other ones too, like a homemade thing made from knotted twine, or a cat collar with a tiny bell on it.

One day they needed to get into groups of two for a project and even though he was usually shy about things like that, he asked her to team up. And she said yes. And then there they were trying to come up with an idea for what to do for it, and one popped into his head. Xavier probably wouldn't have even said it to most people, but, for some reason, with Sasha he didn't even hesitate. "How about we do a thing about a guy who has an adult human body, and the head of a baby. But with a regular adult brain inside. Only because he is a baby, all he can do is cry and cry and cry. Which, like, isn't that what most people want to do all the time, anyway? Because of how life is often very confusing?"

And then Xavier had drawn a little sketch in the corner of his notebook of what this baby-head guy might look like and showed her, and she stared at it and then at him as though maybe they knew each other from a very long time ago and she'd just recognized him. "Yeah," she'd said. "I think that'll work." And when she smiled at him, he felt like he recognized her, too.

The comic they ended up making together was called *The Adventures of Babyhead*. It was basically about how the world is wonderful and terrible, how we are going to die and nothing matters, but it is also beautiful and everything does. That was the theme of their friendship, eventually, the theme of their everything, the underlying current of every interaction they had. Maybe the only thing they were both sure was true.

Xavier thought about all of this, sitting alone in his room on his birthday. He thought about his best friend and how she had been there for him for the whole last horrible month, during which he felt like his chest had been ripped apart by wild animals, or maybe a shark, and that maybe there was no point in leaving his bed ever again. It had surprised him how bad he had felt, how bad he was capable of feeling. But Sasha had not seemed surprised or weirded out or anything, which was another thing he loved about her. She showed up for him, calm and undramatic. She didn't try and make him talk about Ivy, or anything at all. She just came and hung out, even though he knew he was incredibly boring to be around, and he'd say, "Seriously, you can just go home. I am sludge." And she'd tell him to shut his mouth-hole, but always so kindly. She brought him funny mugs she made at her job and they watched all those ocean movies. And she acted like she wasn't even doing him a huge favor, but Xavier knew it took *energy* to be there for someone like that. So what right did Xavier have to just go back to Ivy? To go back to the very person Sasha had saved him from?

He called Sasha. He felt embarrassed and weird and like, without totally meaning to, he was downplaying things, sort of hiding from her a little.

Sasha did not sound happy. And he could tell she was hiding something from him, too, though it was no mystery what it was—she thought he was an idiot. And he wasn't even sure he disagreed with her. He probably was one. He just felt powerless to do anything about it.

When they hung up, his head was kind of spinning. Xavier felt disoriented and strange, and full of energy. After so long of not doing much of anything at all, the idea of sitting still seemed impossible.

He decided to clean up his room. He did laundry and put away all his clothes, swept the floor, made his bed. Then Xavier took out his notebook and drew a picture of some new kind of undersea creature, a cross between a sea lion and an anglerfish with a fancy hat on. Usually Xavier would have taken a photo of it and texted it to Sasha so she could write back some funny caption for it, but somehow in that moment it would have felt wrong, like he would be pretending things were normal between them when they both knew they weren't. That was the problem with being so close to someone, you couldn't bluff your way out of weirdness like that.

When his parents got home, they all sat down to dinner. They gave him a new Moleskine, which they did every year on his birthday, and a gift card for the art store. His dad made tequila chicken tacos and his mom made a spinach salad. His parents were not big talkers, so dinner was mostly quiet, but Xavier could tell that they were glad to see him up and out of bed. There was ice cream for dessert.

Xavier had sort of assumed Sasha would come over to hang

out after dinner. They hadn't talked about it, but he'd just figured, because that's what it had been like most of the summer so far. But then Ivy texted him around eight. Come to the woods. That's all she said. And Xavier felt a little bit weird about it, for a couple of reasons, but Sasha and Xavier hadn't actually had plans. So Xavier went.

This time, Xavier was sober on the walk there and so it was harder to squash down all the thoughts about why he maybe shouldn't be doing this. But then Xavier stepped into the clearing, and there she was, waiting for him on top of a plaid picnic blanket wearing nothing but underwear and boots and leaning back drinking something from a bottle, which she handed to him, and all his concerns vanished. He looked at the label, it was birthday-cake-flavored vodka. He took a sip. Ivy was watching him. She didn't say "Hi" or "Happy birthday" or anything. Just raised her eyebrows, and said "It's cold out here," and then, "Come warm me up."

And so he did.

Afterward she took his face in her hands and she looked him straight in the eye and she said, "Can we please do this for real? Us this? I want to be your girlfriend again."

He wasn't sure how to answer. He wanted to ask, *What's changed? Why now?* But somehow instead he just felt his head nodding yes.

July 23, 1:01 a.m.

Jake: IVY. This is Jake, your brand new boyfriend who lives in your phone

Ivy: This isn't Ivy. Someone gave you a fake number

Ivy: Also, how did you know my name's Ivy?

Jake: Good guess?

Ivy: I already know for a fact you're a very bad guesser. See: the whole hangman thing

Jake: Fair. I guess I saw it in a comment someone posted on one of your photos

Ivy: Creep.

Jake: It's very late. So why aren't you sleeping? Out late with your other boyfriend?

Ivy: HA. I'm awake because of insomnia

Jake: plot twist...your boyfriend's named insomnia?

Ivy: Heh

Jake: So what IS his name?

Ivy: I don't have a boyfriend

Ivy: Why, are you surprised?

Jake: I guess because I don't really expect good things to happen. And to me, this is a good thing, us talking and you being single and all

Jake: Also, I kind of assumed you did from some of your pictures. Who is the guy with the blue hair?

Ivy: He's nobody

Jake: A ghost?

Ivy: No, just nobody important

Ivy: Besides, boys are mostly terrible

Jake: People are mostly terrible

Ivy: PEOPLE are mostly terrible

Jake: jinx

Ivy: JINX

Jake: Well it looks like we agree on one thing, at least

Ivy: What else do we have in common do you think?

Jake: Let's find out . . .

Sasha

The Electric Playhouse was mostly empty. Inside, the air was damp and cool. I had been at the copy shop, printing out a stack of postcards for a book launch, when my phone buzzed with a text from Xavier: Greg is back for 2 days, meeting him and the Mikes at Electric Playhouse. Come by aftr work???

It would be the first time I had seen him since the night before his birthday, which was only four days ago, but after a full month of hanging out basically every day, it felt like years. In the last four days, he and I had only sent about a dozen texts. Meanwhile, I'd exchanged hundreds with his girlfriend. Even earlier that day. Even on the walk over. I had my new second phone shoved down in the bottom of my bag, one of those untraceable pay-as-you-go ones that TV drug dealers use. I got it at the phone store near my job, paid for it with the cash Marc gave me. I felt a little weird about the whole thing—there's a difference between setting up a fake Instagram account drunk at night and buying an actual brand-new phone in the sober day. But I did it. And I was glad. Everything I'd thought about Ivy had so far turned out to be true. She'd take his heart and grind it into dust again, if given the chance. Except this time I'd make sure Xavier wised up before she could.

I walked toward the back, past the snack counter that sold only soft-serve ice cream and stale popcorn, past the prize window where you could redeem your tickets for rubber spiders and plastic gemstone rings, to the section with the vintage arcade games.

There were Greg and Xavier, playing a game called *Night Knight* where knights fight each other in the dark. Neither of them had seen me yet or heard my footsteps over the clanging and banging of the game. Xavier was losing badly.

"Dad's girlfriend thinks American parents are too overprotective, so he had to try and impress her by letting me go off and do whatever I wanted by myself," Greg was saying.

"What'd you do with all your freedom?" Xavier asked.

Greg tapped his joystick quickly. "Went to a couple Italian dance clubs, smooched a fellow or two. Mostly, though, I just went to museums that Dad would have thought were too boring and pondered the great mysteries of the universe." Greg shrugged. "It was good. I can't believe I'm only back for two days, though. How's your summer been so far?"

"Oh, you know, pretty uneventful," Xavier said.

I knew that Xavier and Greg were not the kind of friends who told each other everything, not the kind of friends who had to, but still it was strange to hear him describe his summer as such. Uneventful because he'd never left his bed? Because he'd managed to survive? Because he was back together with a monster?

On the screen, Greg's knight picked Xavier's up off his horse.

"This is painful to watch," I said.

"Hey, kiddo," Greg said.

"He's too good at this game," said Xavier. They were both looking at the screen. He turned to me and our eyes met and my heart pounded. I was used to having a secret from Xavier, but this one felt different. The more secrets you have from someone, the harder it is to look them in the eye. Now, I could barely look at him at all.

Off to the side a couple of kids were standing at the top of the Skee-Ball machine, and dropping the balls though a hole in the netting directly into the five-hundred-point hole.

"Hey, no worries if you don't want to discuss, but Little Mike said he and Big Mike haven't seen you all summer. They told me about you and Ivy and the whole thing. That's rough. You okay?"

"Yeah, I mean . . . It was crappy there for a minute." Xavier's ears were turning red. "I'm fine now, though. Actually, about Ivy, we're . . ."

My entire body was tingling. Maybe now was going to be my chance to say the thing I needed to say. To do the thing I needed to do. On the game screen, Greg's knight was about to knock off Xavier's knight's helmet.

"Sasha, do you want to step in and save your buddy here?" Greg said. "I am *crushing* him."

I bumped Xavier out of the way and took over the controls. A few seconds later, the victory music played and the game was over.

"Sorry," Greg said. "You never stood a chance." He turned toward me. We hugged hello.

"Greg picked up an Australian accent in Europe," Xavier said.

"It's true, mate," Greg said.

I nodded, deadpan. "Makes sense."

I went to the change machine and got quarters. Big Mike and Little Mike arrived. There was lots of hugging and high-fiving. Everybody was into Xavier's blue hair and agreed I had done a very good job. These boys weren't my friends, but I liked them. They were nice people and easy to be around. I thought of them as simple, but not in a bad way.

We played *Gauntlet* and *Q*bert* and *Tetris*, and all the while I felt my new phone buzzing in my bag. Little Mike played some ten-year-old at *Space Invaders* and lost. Big Mike hit the jackpot on a game where you spin a wheel and won one hundred tickets, and for a minute, while excitedly watching the tickets come out, he looked like a giant kid, which was sweet.

When we ran out of quarters, we got soft-serve and sodas and sat at this one big picnic table in the back.

We talked about random things: movies, a robotics course the Mikes were taking at a local college, a girl who Little Mike had a crush on, and whether or not the Electric Playhouse was a front for some kind of organized crime thing, because it somehow remained in business even though hardly anyone was ever in there.

"Hey," Greg said to Xavier. "Before—weren't you starting to say something about Ivy?"

I sat straight up, adrenaline buzzing.

"About how she's a total jerk?" Big Mike said. He turned to me. "My sister said that insults shouldn't be related to gender. So that's why I didn't call her a bitch."

Xavier looked down. "Well, it's just . . . we're sort of seeing each other again. We're back together, I guess. . . ."

"Oh!" Greg took a sip of his soda. "How'd that happen?"

"I bumped into her. Well, me and Sasha both did. And it just . . . y'know."

"Whoa," Big Mike said. "Sorry I called your girlfriend a jerk."

Little Mike said, "Are you happy?"

"Yeah, I think I am."

"Well, then," Greg said, "if you're happy, we're happy." He smiled. They were all smiling. I wondered how many details

Xavier had told them about his and Ivy's relationship the first time around. None of them had really spent any time with her.

"Yes, that's right," said Big Mike. "As our only son, your happiness is paramount."

Little Mike turned to me, and stage-whispered, "He's not actually my only son. But don't tell his mom." Then he winked. And that was that.

Big Mike stood up. "I'm going to get more quarters," he said. "*Tetris* time?"

"You should check her phone," I blurted out. They all looked up at me.

"Whose?" said Greg.

"Ivy's," I said. "Xavier should." I turned toward him. "If you're going to be back together with her, then you shouldn't blindly trust her. You should look at her phone."

"You mean like spy on her?" Big Mike said.

"Not *spy*," I said. I felt my face turning red. I had meant to sound casual. This was so important, and I was fucking it up. "Just look at her phone to see if she's up to anything with other guys."

"Isn't that messed up, though?" Little Mike said.

They were all staring at me, except Xavier, who was looking at the bottom of his empty soft-serve ice-cream cup.

"So is cheating," I said. "If you're going be with her, you have to at least make sure that . . . Well, you just have to look at her phone. To see what she's doing. I mean, considering everything from before . . . Because didn't you say that with the other guy, that they'd been texting? Right?" My words were jumbling themselves up inside my mouth. I felt weird even revealing those details in front of his other friends, maybe he hadn't even told them. But I had to keep going. He had to hear this. "Because the guy said something to her about the texts? So if she's going to do it again, her phone would be a good place to look. . . ."

"Maybe you're right," Xavier said to me. His face was red, too. "Maybe I will. Okay?" But I wasn't sure if he even meant it or if he was just trying to get me to stop.

Greg went and got three more dollars in quarters and they played a few more games. When the quarters ran out, we all said our goodbyes. Xavier's phone buzzed, and I figured he must be going to meet Ivy from the way he was not quite looking at me as he left.

July 26, 1:48 a.m.

Ivy: CAN'T

Ivy: SLEEP

Ivy: PPPP

Ivy: PP

Ivy: PPPPP

Ivy: And yes I sent so many texts in a row, because I am VERY SELFISH and was hoping all the text bings would WAKE YOU UP

Ivy: Did it work!?!?

Jake: Ha. HA! Ha ha. It didn't work

Jake: Because I was already awake

Jake: And I keep my phone on vibrate

Jake: Hi

Ivy: HI

Ivy: I have a question for you . . . remember the other day when you asked me if I have a boyfriend? I realized I didn't ask you: Do YOU have a GIRLFRIEND?

Jake: No

Jake: Would you mind if I did?

Ivy: Honestly?

Jake: Of course honestly. There's no reason to lie

Ivy: Then yes. I would mind. Does that sound stupid?

Jake: No. I wouldn't want you to have a boyfriend either

Ivy: So why DON'T you have a girlfriend?

Jake: Honestly?

Ivy: 😬

Jake: I don't do relationships

Ivy: Why not?

Jake: Mostly I just like to make out with people and then . . . not date them

Ivy: How come?

Jake: I guess because I pretty much never like anyone

Ivy: . . . because most people are IDIOTS. I get that. I AGREE

Ivy: But not everyone is

Jake: no, not everyone

Ivy: Have you ever been in love?

Ivy: Am I allowed to ask that?

Jake: You can ask me anything

Jake: And . . . yes, I have been. Once

Ivy: what was it like?

Jake: It was like someone stuck a fist into my chest and just kept grabbing around in there until my heart got caught. Pretty fucking painful mostly

Ivy: I thought falling in love was supposed to be MAGICAL

Jake: I guess it depends on the details

Jake: Have you been?

Ivy: No

Jake: Really? Never?

Ivy: Never not ever

Jake: Do you want to be?

Ivy: Are you PROPOSITIONING me?

Jake: I'm DARING you

Jake: What are you so scared of?

Ivy: I'm not scared of anything

Jake: liar

Ivy: Um . . . did you just call me a liar?

Jake: Oh shoot, sorry that was a typo

Jake: What I meant was . . .

Jake: REALLY BIG LIAR

Ivy: wtf!

Jake: Either you're lying to me or you're lying to yourself, or you're lying to both of us

Ivy: Dude, you barely know me

Jake: I bet I know you better than you think

Jake: Look, all I'm saying is everyone is scared of something, and the people who claim not to be are usually the most scared of all

Ivy: All right smartass, what am I so scared of?

Jake: Oh I dunno. Well like you said, I don't REALLY know you . . . but if I had to guess I'd guess you're scared of

Jake: losing control

Jake: or being out of control

Jake: of people knowing who you really are

Jake: And maybe you're scared that nothing matters and maybe you're equally scared that everything does, and you just want to tell yourself nothing matters so you don't have to take responsibility for your own actions and life

Jake: like sure it sucks if nothing matters . . . but at least then you're free from having to try and DO anything . . .

Jake: Yknow, or something

Jake: you still there??

Ivy: I can't decide if I'm mad at you for being such a cocky asshole . . . or if I love you now

Jake: probably a little of both

Jake: Does that mean you think I'm right?

Ivy: I don't know what it means

Jake: In your regular life, no one ever contradicts you, huh. You have everyone convinced you're really a tough fearless badass

Ivy: Something like that. How did you know?

Jake: Just a feeling I guess

Ivy: So what are YOU scared of??

Ivy: . . .

Ivy: . . .

Ivy: Jake?

Sasha

The truth was, back at the very beginning, before I learned enough about Ivy to hate her, before I felt how I later would about Xavier, I actually thought she and I might become friends.

It was early February. Xavier and Ivy had been hooking up for only a few weeks. "I think you'll really like each other" is what Xavier had said. And then he suggested the three of us hang out. "You'll probably like each other better than you both like me!"

It had been a bright, cold afternoon when we went to get nachos at a place you could walk to from school. Xavier was talking fast and kept making cringey nacho jokes the whole way over. "Na-cho nachos! My nachos!" I knew he was just nervous because he really wanted it to go well. I laughed at his jokes, tried to make him relax. Ivy was irritated and made no effort to hide it. "Dude, cut back on the coffee," she'd said, but without even a hint of a smirk.

After that, Ivy barely spoke. She rolled her eyes at everything Xavier said, and ignored me entirely. Halfway through the nachos, which only I was eating, Ivy got up to say hi to some people she knew. A few minutes later, Xavier got a funny look on his face, and I turned around and saw that Ivy was sitting on some guy's lap. Xavier had tried to shrug it off. "Oh, that's just a friend of hers," he said quickly. But his face was pink and he looked away.

Later, Xavier had said maybe things were weird when we all hung out because Ivy and I were too similar. "You're both tough and no-bullshit kind of people," he'd said. "So it makes sense you wouldn't click at first. Guess you need a softie like me to glue you together." He smiled. And then explained that apart from her best friend, Gwen, Ivy wasn't usually friends with girls. "You realize how messed up that is," I said to him. "You're not friends with girls, either," he said. "But that's because I'm not friends with anyone," I said, then paused. "Except for you." Xavier said he was sure it would be less awkward the next time. Only there never really was a next time.

My feelings started to change soon after, but still, if Ivy had been nice to Xavier, been kind to him, I would have put my own feelings aside. I would have put my own feelings aside and been happy that my friend was happy, even if seeing him with someone else made me feel like I'd been kicked in the stomach.

But Ivy wasn't good.

She would get drunk and say mean things. Or she would flirt outrageously in front of him, pretend he was imagining it, and somehow convince him he was.

And then of course, there was the vanishing thing.

The very first time she'd done it was six weeks after they first started seeing each other. One day, they had plans and she just didn't show up. Xavier called me, insane with worry, certain something terrible had happened to her. He wanted to call her parents but didn't have their number, so he went over to her house. No one was home, and this scared him even more. Maybe her parents were already with her at the hospital! What other reason could there be? Ivy finally texted him twelve torturous hours later: I forgot we had plans and my phone was out of batteries. You are a sweetie to have been worried. And Xavier was so very happy and relieved.

She did it again a couple weeks later. That time she claimed she had food poisoning and couldn't get to her phone. "But how hard is it to send a text?" I had asked. "She was really sorry," Xavier said, as though that explained it.

The next time, she didn't even have an excuse, was just full of self-hatred, offering no explanation other than her tears. She didn't *know* why she did it, she said. Maybe it was because of her controlling parents—she needed to know she didn't have to answer to anyone. But she swore it wouldn't happen again. And when it did, Xavier forgave her then, too.

Xavier told me, whenever Ivy did anything maybe not that great to him, she was always *so* upset about it after that he just ended up wanting to comfort her. I had overheard him doing it on the phone more than once, talking to her in these sweet, gentle tones, telling her please, please not to worry about it, that everything was just fine. It always filled me with anger and longing in equal measure.

How could he be mad at her, he said, when she was already so mad at herself?

I thought it was a pretty messed-up trick, using her self-flagellation as a way to excuse herself of anything. But it worked.

After a while, Xavier stopped telling me the details of their relationship. We were still in touch all the time, sending drawings (his) and stories (mine) back and forth by text, and we still hung out, watched animal movies and ate too much candy and tried to teach ourselves magic tricks from YouTube videos or whatever. But we basically stopped talking about Ivy, even though I knew he thought about her pretty much all the time.

There is this parasite I had read about once. If a rat catches it, it makes them love the smell of cat piss. They love that smell of cat piss so much that they just hang out wherever cats have been peeing, all happy and drugged up and loved up on all that cat piss, until the cat comes, pounces, and kills them dead. That's what it was like with Xavier and Ivy. It was like Xavier had a brain disease and there was no hope for him.

"I know she can be a weirdo," Xavier had said to me once. "I love her, though, that's the problem." Then he smiled, resigned.

I had wanted to tell him that loving someone should never *be* a problem, should never feel like one, but by then I already knew firsthand it wasn't really that simple.

July 31, 4:08 p.m.

Jake: why do you text me so much

Ivy: What do you mean?

Jake: I mean all day long we text text text a million times a day and have been for the past ten days. I just crunched the numbers here and that's 10 million texts, which is a lot

Ivy: Well why do YOU text ME so much?

Jake: You can't just repeat my question with DIFFERENT EMPHASIS

Ivy: OH can't I?

Jake: I guess you CAN

Ivy: The full truth? I feel like you're a voice in my head now. And it's less lonely in my brain with you in there. So instead of thinking thinking thinking, I say hello

Jake: What was in there before? In your brain?

Ivy: JUST SCREAMING

Ivy: Really though, it was just my own mean thoughts rattling around in there. My brain made them all

Jake: It's lonely to be trapped inside your own brain all the time

Ivy: Is that a question or a statement?

Jake: A statement

Ivy: So then we agree

Jake: I guess we do

Ivy: PLOT TWIST: you're not even real

Ivy: I made you up

Jake: Or maybe I made YOU up

Jake: See what I did there?

Ivy: now I know you're real . . . if I made you up, you'd have better jokes

Jake: Mean!

Ivy: KIDDING!

Ivy: I guess the truth is, I can be my real self with you

Ivy: I literally cannot ever do that with anyone

Ivy: Even people who think I'm close to them . . . I'm not REALLY honest

Ivy: Even with my supposed best friend

Ivy: I'm who she wants me to be when I'm with her

Ivy: Because it's easier

Ivy: THAT IS SO CORNY I THREW UP

Ivy: I think you are not not not not not not not not not not not terrible

Ivy: Which is to say, pretty damn good

Ivy: And I literally never tell anyone that

Ivy: I don't believe in luck

Ivy: But I feel very lucky to have found you

Ivy: DELETE THIS IF ANYONE EVER SAW THIS IT WOULD RUIN MY REP

Jake: Deleted. Your secret is safe with me

Ivy: Thank you

Ivy: SO YOU BETTER NOT FUCK THIS UP!

Xavier

A week and a half after Xavier's birthday, Ivy invited him to a party. Actually what she said was, "Some people are going to get fucked up at this guy Nikolai's. He has a pool. Maybe if we're lucky, someone will drown and we can watch."

When Ivy and Xavier were together the first time around, there was always somebody else's house, liquor stolen from a cabinet or a box in a basement or bought by an older brother. There were things to smoke, pills to take, sometimes something to snort (though Xavier never did). Always a group of people that Ivy somehow knew and Xavier didn't. And they were constantly inviting her places, and Ivy would say she was totally not in a mood to see any of them, but then she'd go anyway because she wanted alcohol or drugs, or a way to kill time. "I know one million people but have no friends at all," Ivy said once. "No one cares about me, and I don't care about them, either . . .

except for you." "What about Gwen?" Xavier had said. "She's your best friend." And then he immediately felt embarrassed because probably she'd been kidding. But she just shrugged, and said, "Gwen's not a friend. . . ." His heart beat hard. Xavier was sometimes scared by how easily she could discard people. Only then she finished with, "she's family."

Xavier thought Nikolai might have been someone Ivy had hooked up with when he and Ivy were apart. He wasn't sure exactly why he thought that. Maybe it was the way she said his name. Xavier could imagine her saying it naked. But he tried not to. Sometimes it's better not to imagine anything at all.

What was notable about this party, though, wasn't the Nikolai part. It was that after Ivy had told him about it, she'd said, "Hey, why don't you bring your buddy along?" And Xavier knew she meant Sasha. The idea made Xavier nervous, even though he was sure it was a good thing. Stuff had been increasingly weird between him and Sasha ever since his birthday. They hadn't been hanging out nearly as much as usual, though they still texted sometimes, but only sometimes. And the tone was different. Have you looked at Ivy's phone yet? was the last one he'd gotten from her. She'd sent it a full twenty-four hours before and he hadn't responded because he didn't know what to say. It was hard to go back to regular joking after something like that.

The day of the party, the black clouds rolled in thick and heavy, hanging low enough to crush you. When the storm finally broke, there would be a six-car pileup on the interstate that would kill a boy that none of them had ever met or heard of, but whose face would be plastered all over the news, until someone else's face appeared to replace it. But they didn't know any of that yet. Later, Xavier would look back on this night, searching for clues of what was to come. Looking for hints of the future in the way the day played out. But the actual danger was lurking so deep beneath the surface, they never saw it coming.

It was over ninety by midmorning. There was a heat advisory in effect and a storm warning, and nothing felt real. Ivy texted him to let him know the party was still on. Maybe lightning will hit the pool and someone will FRY, she wrote. I'll get you at 7. I don't want to miss anything.

Sasha texted, too. Meet you there. Hope it doesn't rain. I want to swim around and look for sea creatures

Ivy was late picking him up, and by the time they got to the party, the place was already crowded. Nikolai's parents seemed to be very rich—there was a massive in-ground pool with a hot tub, a trampoline, a tennis court, and a giant open lawn. There were beach chairs everywhere, grouped in twos and threes, and a huge table under a big umbrella off to one side.

"I bet his mommy's medicine cabinet is *stocked the fuck up*," Ivy said, then grabbed Xavier's hand and headed straight for the drinks table.

And that's when Xavier spotted Sasha.

There she was, lounging in a beach chair in that red-and-white polka-dot bathing suit she always wore, holding a beer, and watching the crowd. If Xavier had been invited to a party where he knew only one person, he'd have made sure to get there after they did, so he wouldn't be alone. But Sasha just didn't care about things like that, which Xavier so admired and was so perplexed by. As she watched the party, Xavier watched her. The funny thing about spending a ton of time with someone is that eventually you can't really tell what they look like. Your brain just fills in what you already know. But suddenly, it was like she was a brand-new person he'd never seen before. She looked powerful and strong and solid. She was beautiful.

Sasha glanced up and spotted them. Xavier waved and held up a finger like *there in a sec*, and she shrugged and smiled and did a bunch of hand motions in a row. A thumbs-up, the *check please* motion. She gave herself bunny ears and used her thumb to give her fist a mouth. For a moment, it felt like the past weird week and a half had never even happened.

Xavier turned back toward Ivy and realized she'd been watching him watch Sasha. She grabbed a beer off the table, took three quick gulps, and then topped the bottle off with rum.

"Let's go say hi to your friend," Ivy said. She stuck her phone into one of her bathing-suit straps, gulped her drink, and started walking toward Sasha. She looked determined in a way that filled his stomach with cold dread. He tried to shake it off. This was a *good thing*, he reminded himself. It would be good if they became friends.

Ivy and Sasha had never quite clicked the first time around, but it was his own fault, Xavier knew. The one time the three of them had hung out, he was so nervous he babbled away like an idiot and made it awkward for everyone. And after that he'd told Sasha too many stories about Ivy that probably didn't make her sound so great. But now things could be different. Xavier just needed to step back, to give them a chance.

Ivy leaned down to hug Sasha. "So glad you came," Ivy said.

"Me too," Sasha said. "This place is . . ." She looked around.

"Absurd, right? I think his parents are oil barons or something. Cute suit."

"Oh thanks . . . I like your bracelets." She motioned to the big jangly stacks on Ivy's wrists.

Ivy grinned. "They're so heavy, it's like I'm doing a little workout every time I move my arms." She did a pumping-iron motion. Sasha laughed. And Xavier felt his insides uncoil. Ivy was really trying. Both of them were. "So how's your summer going?" she went on. "Xavier said you've been working at . . ."

Xavier stood there while they talked. He felt himself starting to smile.

A couple minutes later, Ivy held her beer bottle upside down. A few drops spilled out onto the ground. "Let's get another one."

Ivy grabbed Xavier by the arm and pulled him over to another table full of drinks. "Hey," Xavier said. He took Ivy's hand and squeezed it. "Thank you so much for . . ."

But Ivy wasn't listening. "What do you think?" she said. She nodded at Sasha and then motioned toward three guys sitting in lawn chairs near her. Xavier couldn't hear what they were saying, but he got the general gist from the way they were looking at her. Xavier felt immediately protective. Not that Sasha needed protection.

"You mean what do I think about those creeps?" Xavier asked.

Ivy grinned.

"I think Sasha should date one of them," Ivy said. "Or at least fuck them."

"That's . . . ," Xavier started to say. But he had no idea what it was.

Ivy leaned over to reach into one of the coolers. Her phone slid out of her bathing-suit top and onto the pavement with a *thunk*. She stared at it confused, and that's when Xavier realized she was already a little buzzed. He got the phone for her. There was a crack in the corner of the screen. "Oh no," Xavier said. Ivy snatched it from him and stuck it in her pocket.

"I want her to fuck one of them so she can stop being so obsessed with you. It's honestly incredibly pathetic."

"Whoa . . . what are you talking about?"

Ivy shrugged, then leaned over again, and pulled out a coconut seltzer. She splashed half out onto the ground and filled the can back up with rum.

"She wants to climb your dick," Ivy said. She gulped her drink.

It took a while for his brain to process the words she was saying.

Ivy smirked. "Sasha's a total psycho about you, and don't pretend you don't know it."

Xavier knew Ivy got sort of crazy when she was drunk sometimes, would get into this reckless mood where she might just say anything. But this seemed different somehow. She wasn't *that* drunk. And she sounded so calm, and like she genuinely meant what she was saying.

His stomach flipped.

"I have no idea where you're even getting this from," Xavier said. "She doesn't . . ." He paused. "We don't think about each other like that. Not even a little."

Ivy took her phone out again and looked down at it. "Why do you think she's even here?" She started scrolling through her messages, as though this was just a casual conversation.

"She's here because you invited her," Xavier said. "And you were just being *nice* to each other." His blood was pumping in his ears.

Ivy shook her head. "Couldn't you tell that neither of us meant it? She's here because you are a magnet for her pussy and she will follow you wherever you go. Also she doesn't like me and she wants to check up on us."

"Stop!" Xavier said. He turned to look for Sasha, to make sure she was out of earshot. But she wasn't in her chair anymore. Where was she? "She'll hear you."

But Ivy kept going. "She's not exactly *slick* about it. I know what she's up to. Have you seen the way she looks at you?" She stuck her tongue through her teeth, and curled her lip. "It's so gross and weird and sad. You can practically smell her pussy juicing when she sees you. Spreading like a flow-er, dripping into that dumb bathing suit that is too small for her weird body."

"Jesus Christ, Ivy!" Xavier said.

He turned again. Sasha was heading for the diving board, her face completely calm. She hadn't heard, he decided, but his relief was quickly replaced by anger. He felt it fizzling hot in his stomach, so unfamiliar that he didn't even know what it was at first. Xavier had never really been mad at Ivy before. Even when she'd cheated on him, he'd only been hurt and sad. But now . . . He clenched his jaw. "She's my best friend," he said. His voice was low and he barely sounded like himself. "And there is nothing between us, and she has never been anything but nice to you, so *do not talk* about her like that to me. Ever again. EVER. I mean it."

Ivy was smiling ever so slightly as she dumped the rest of her drink down her throat. "I'm just messing around," Ivy said. "Sorry, okay? Seriously, I'm sorry. That was out of line. I'm just a little drunk and saying dumb things I don't even mean, okay?" She grabbed the rum again and took a swig straight from the bottle. "You've never talked to me like that before, though." Ivy looked him up and down slowly, looked at his hands, tightly gripped around the back of a deck chair, at his narrowed eyes, and his gritted teeth. Then stepped toward him, grinning. "Not bad . . ."

Sasha

I climbed to the top of the diving board. Bounced once, twice, jumped, splashed, sank. Only when I was underwater did I let myself scream.

Fuck.

Ivy.

Fuck.

Fuck.

Fuck.

Ivy.

Ivy had known I could hear her. She'd *wanted* me to hear her—she was staring at me over Xavier's shoulder the entire time. When she said the word "pussy," we'd locked eyes. She'd *smiled*.

And Xavier had no idea.

I pushed off the bottom of the pool. When my face broke through the water, I took a deep gasping breath.

But Ivy was wrong about one thing. She said she knew just what I was up to.

She had no fucking clue.

My eyes tingled as the tears collected. Because under the anger was something else, something so embarrassing I could barely even admit it to myself: in the past ten days, *I had actually started to like her.*

I had felt as though maybe I'd been getting to see some secret hidden piece of her. Maybe all along she had been covering up the most real part of herself. Like so many of us. Like even me sometimes.

But more than that, worse than that, worse than anything ...

There had been times late at night, when I was by myself in my house, in my bed, and texts from Ivy had made me feel less alone.

I pressed on my eyelids, forced the tears back in.

It was fucking pathetic.

I looked around. I was the only one in the pool. The three guys who'd been talking about me in the grossest ways were in chairs near the edge, watching me. Did *anyone* at this party other than Ivy understand how sound travels? That other people have *ears*?

I pulled myself out.

"Wish she'd jump off the diving board again," one of them said. "Jump for a real long time."

I made my way toward them, slowly, calmly. They nudged one

another. One smiled at me. I didn't smile back. "Shut the fuck up or the next thing I jump on will be your fucking skull," I said. The idiots stared at me, openmouthed. I turned and walked away.

I wanted to leave then, to go home to my empty house. To crank up the AC and climb under the covers.

Instead I forced myself to breathe. I headed for the drinks table. I cracked a beer. My hands were shaking. I wanted them to stop shaking. The party was more crowded than before. The music was louder. There was a splash as someone jumped into the pool. A scream and another splash as a girl pushed her friend in in all her clothes. I gritted my teeth, sipped the beer. It tasted like dirt. So I gulped. I looked left and right.

I told myself I would not be sad. I would feel nothing but anger now.

People act like being angry is a bad thing. Calm down, sit down, be quiet, be a good girl.

Fuck. That.

Anger is power. Anger is a weapon and a gift. Anger takes the pit in your stomach and makes it a black hole. And everybody *watch the fuck out.*

I looked for Ivy. She was standing with Xavier, checking her phone. I knew just what she was checking for.

And in that moment I realized what I'd originally planned wouldn't be enough. It wouldn't be enough for Xavier to figure out that Ivy was texting with Jake, then dump her, and be safe and free. No.

I wanted Ivy to suffer.

I wanted to watch her face when she found out that I was the one she'd been telling all her secrets to. I wanted to watch her perfect mask crumble and fall.

I looked around the yard. There were maybe forty people here now. I felt brave and reckless. I felt like I could say or do anything. I knew what I needed then, a body pressed against mine, a mouth on my mouth. Something intense and sudden, to keep me from having to think about what Ivy had said, what Xavier had said in response, to keep me from having to replay that conversation over and over and over in my head until the words were carved so deep into my brain I would never be able to get them out.

There was a girl in a blue-striped bikini standing at the edge of the pool, tall with smooth skin and a soft sexy belly squishing over the waistband of her suit. I took a sip of my beer and started toward her. With guys, it was simple. I knew just how to do it, how to approach them, the smirk, the look. I was less confident with girls, but in that moment I didn't care.

"Hey," someone called out. "Hey, Sasha!"

I turned and there was Gwen. I watched as she drank from a plastic water bottle, flinched, and passed it to a guy next to her who took a sip and chased it with a swig of Sprite. He caught my eye and smiled. I'd seen him around before. Steph was his name, I thought. I glanced at the girl with the striped bikini. She had her arm around a guy now and he was kissing her on the neck.

I looked back at Steph. He held the bottle up like, *Want some?*
He didn't have to ask me twice.

Thirty minutes later the water bottle, which had been filled with
gin, was empty. And everything was different.

"You remember our song, right?" Gwen was saying. I shook
my head, grinning. "How did it go?" She started to hum *Frère
Jacques*, then leaned in and whisper-sang the words we'd made
up. *"Bon-jour, mon-sieur, mon-sieur le butt,"* and just like that it
all came rushing back. We'd made up new lyrics, a mix of fake
French words and butt words. There was a dance that went
with it. Our eyes met and I honked an imaginary butt in the
air, part of the dance, and she laughed. It felt good, sitting there
laughing with someone at the party. For a moment, I could
almost forget everything that was going on. Almost. "We were
such little psychos," I said.

"Were?" she said. And we laughed some more. She turned
toward Steph. "We wrote a song in French about butts. We were
very sophisticated nine-year-olds."

His knee was touching mine—it had been for a while.
I looked up at him. *An accident?* He was staring out at the
water. He turned to meet my eye.

"Is there a video of this around somewhere?" he said.
"Feels like a missed opportunity that you didn't become viral
Internet superstars."

"It's truly unfair that there isn't," Gwen said.

Steph moved forward, so now our legs were side by side, the outside of his thigh sliding up the outside of mine. I did not pull away.

Suddenly there was a loud banging, a drumbeat. Someone had changed the music and cranked it up, up, up. Then came the flute, an electric violin, an otherworldly voice. I turned toward the sound. Everyone did. And there was Ivy, switching on the extra speakers, a tiny smile played at her lips.

She walked slowly around the edge of the pool, made her way onto a small square of soft grass. She was alone. The sun was going down. My heart thumped hard.

"She's a pretty fucked-up person, you know," Gwen said.

"Sorry?" I said. Gwen was watching me watching Ivy. "I thought she was your best friend."

"She is," Gwen said. "Which means I know her better than anyone, and I know who she is deep down. And who she is is completely messed up." Gwen's face was expressionless. It was hard to tell if she meant this in a good way or a bad one.

"How so?" I said.

Gwen raised an eyebrow. "All the ways you think. And other ones, too." She shrugged, then turned back to watch Ivy, and so did I.

Steph's leg was still touching mine, but I couldn't feel it anymore. By the pink glow of the setting sun, to the sound of drums and flutes and voice, Ivy began to dance.

She turned like a ballerina, around and around. She

crouched low and popped back up, eyes closed, chest out, head thrown back. She brought one leg up in front of her, higher and higher until her thigh pressed against her torso. The music was loud and fast, but she moved so slowly now, graceful, like she was underwater.

She didn't dance like no one was watching. She danced like she knew we all would be.

And she was right—the whole party was staring, caught in a trance. I turned to Xavier, my sweet best friend, who was leaning forward, lip bit, and I thought, *I get it*. And I understood then that I would never forget this moment, not because of what she said, not because I hated her, not even because of the look on Xavier's face, but just because it was so goddamn beautiful.

Finally, the song ended. Another one came on, softer. Ivy stopped, her body glistening with sweat. She walked back toward the pool, took off her shorts, and dove in.

The girl in the striped bikini was standing at the edge. "What song was that?" she asked.

"Finbeeyato," Ivy said.

"By who?"

"By Monster Hands."

"Who are they?" said the girl.

But Ivy didn't answer, she had dunked underwater and was gone.

* * *

The party lasted forever. Eventually the clouds darkened and gathered close and blocked out all the stars. Lightning cracked and the rain came down. We got drunker and drunker. Here's how the night ended: me and Steph around the side of the house under a wraparound porch, his lips against mine, hands fumbling into each other's bathing suits while the water pounded down. When I told him it was time for me to leave, he begged and begged me not to. "We don't even have to do anything," he said. "You're just so cool . . . I want to hang out more. We can find a dry place to talk."

I shrugged and pulled away. "Sorry," I said.

"What about hanging out a different time?" he said. "Like other than now?" He looked at me like I was very precious and was about to disappear. "Could I have your phone number?"

He handed me his phone. There was a loud crack of lightning and a *Woo!* from the pool. I punched the numbers in, not even sure why I was doing it. I had no intention of seeing him again. Maybe because I was drunk. Maybe I wanted to pretend I was just a normal person doing normal things at a party. Maybe it was because by the end of the night I felt powerful and reckless. Like I could do anything. And no one could stop me.

"You can text me," I said. I put in my last digit, added my name as SASHA WHO HATES TALKING ON THE PHONE. And when I handed his phone back, he was looking at me like I was magic.

August 2, 2:06 a.m.

Jake: When we meet, I'll play this song for you in person. For now, there's something I need you to look up

Jake: It's Finbeeyato by this band called Monster Hands

Jake: Is it weird to say I'm sure you will love it even though I have actually no idea what music you like?

Jake: If that's weird, instead let's pretend I said: here's a song. No pressure to like it

Jake: It reminds me of you. I don't know why

Jake: Sorry for the longest text chain on earth. I'm a lil drunk

Jake: I guess you'll see this in the morning

Jake: Good morning

Ivy: 1. Well you were right that I'd love it, I already DO love it.

I've been listening to it on repeat for the past week. Are you living inside my brain?

Ivy: 2. GET OUT OF MY BRAIN

Ivy: 3. No, I'm just kidding. Stay in here. Someone needs to be the chaperone

Ivy: 4. WHEN WE MEET? Are you serious? Do not mess with me Jake. I thought you said we couldn't. I thought you were too shy . . .

Jake: What are you still doing up?

Jake: 1. Maybe I'm living inside your brain or maybe I AM you. And you've been writing to yourself all along. Did you ever think about THAT?

Jake: 2. NEVER

Jake: 3. Oh, okay good. I'm glad you were kidding. Because I was serious when I said it before. I will say it again: N E V E R

Jake: 4. I know, I was shy, I AM shy. But there are some things worth taking risks for . . . don't you think?? SO YES I AM SERIOUS

Jake: And by the way . . . get to bed young lady

Ivy: Come over and make me

Ivy: PS good

Here's the thing about the messages: they were just supposed to be a distraction, a joke, a game for my brain to play while I wait to die. I'm sorry I do not mean to be so DRAMATIC here. I am just a realistic person who is not too scared to admit that that is what all of life is: a bunch of activities we do in a row to pass the time until there is no more time for us to pass.

Look, I am not a dummy. I know how that sounds. I am extremely, fully aware that people are DISTURBED when you talk like that. You have to be careful about who you say things to when you know this. People have a hard time accepting it. It makes them feel BAD, so they decide that knowing the truth is actually a symptom of a DISEASE, as a way to convince themselves that this upsetting truth isn't just true.

I got forced to go to a shrink once, a long time ago. I thought WELL better to talk than sit there in silence. So I expressed this viewpoint, this very true viewpoint, before I understood that it is always better to keep this to yourself. The shrink said I was depressed. I said, "I'm not depressed, I am RIGHT. Can you argue with anything I'm saying? Can you really tell me how anything matters at all and how doing one thing is different than doing another thing if in the end there will just be nothing, anyway??" I was not crying. I was not even frowning. I was smiling, actually, if I recall. Because it was during school hours and I was getting out of a math test.

She said to me you do not need to feel sad to be depressed. She said are you thinking about killing yourself? I said NO I am not thinking about KILLING MYSELF. She said but if you were how would you do it? And I said what the hell, are you looking for IDEAS? She said I am only checking that you are not lying when you say you are not. I said lordy, if I were trying to lie do you really think you'd get me with your clever THEORETICAL question trick? She looked for a moment very tired, like I was exhausting her. She said well that sounds like depressed to me. I said no I am not depressed, I am not even sad. I am just smart and RIGHT. She said depression lies to you. I said EVERYBODY LIES TO YOU. She said who has lied to you lately and I said I did not even want to get into that. Then we sat there in silence until she said my time was up. I took more than a reasonable amount of gummy bears from the bowl on her table. (What kind of shrink has gummy bears in her office I ask you? Maybe she was colluding with the dentist whose office was down the hall, eh?) And I got the hell out of there.

I learned to fake it better after that. I learned to pretend JUST ENOUGH so that no one would worry. Just enough so that I could go about my life without people bothering me. (And I get it, I get that they were WELL MEANING, but in the end, in a hundred and fifty years, this entire planet will be hosting a new big shitty party full of people and nothing we did or did not do or meant or did not mean will have mattered.)

I am not trying to be fake-deep here. I know that nothing I'm saying is new. What I'm trying to explain is that I really, truly did not think that anything that MATTERED could happen when we started writing each other, because I did not think anything COULD matter. I did not think mattering was a REAL THING.

It was just WORDS at first, WORDS WORDS WORDS, an exercise really. But then somehow something changed and I felt like something was HAPPENING with me and Jake. IT felt like he was (get ready to barf) seeing INSIDE me somehow. It was like there was something even in there to see. And I didn't feel like I was pretending. I had gotten SO GOOD at pretending, but suddenly it didn't feel like I had to (well, not in the big ways at least).

I waited for that feeling to pass. I did not TRUST IT. I waited for it to GO. But every morning I went to sleep with it. And every morning when I woke up, there it was, like some soft small animal next to my bed.

When I started out, nothing mattered. I was as sure of it as I was sure of anything. But the problem is now I have something to care about. Which, as it turns out, is so wonderful and so goddamn terrifying.

But the truth, the fucking truth, could ruin everything.

Sasha

Xavier and I hardly ever talked on the phone. Other than the call on his birthday, I couldn't even remember the last time we had. So when I saw his name flashing on my screen the morning after Nikolai's party, my first thought was that maybe something bad had happened.

"Hello?" I sat up, suddenly dizzy.

"Oh, hi there," he said. He sounded kind of normal.

"Is something terribly wrong?" I asked. "Are you dead?"

"Let me check," he said. "How would I know?"

"Is your heart still beating?"

"There's something thumping around in my chest, but I can't say for sure what it is. . . ."

I thought about the night before. What Ivy had said to him, what he'd said back. I felt my face flush. I was glad he couldn't see me.

"Why are you calling me?" I said. "We don't talk on the phone."

It came out harsher than I'd meant it.

"Oh, I don't know," he said. "I guess I just thought we might try it. It's not like the very first time or anything."

"Okay," I said.

"So how do you think this is going?" he said.

"I'm not sure yet," I said. "I don't talk to people on the phone, except when people call the shop. I have nothing to compare it to. And you haven't yet ordered any copies."

I got out of bed. It was 9:26. My head was pounding. I had to be at work in thirty-four minutes.

"Did you have fun last night?" His voice sounded strange and, it occurred to me then that maybe he was calling because he was worried I'd overheard him and Ivy at the party. Maybe he was calling to check.

"Yeah," I said. And then, just in case, I added, "It was fun to get to hang out with Ivy a little bit." The only thing worse than my overhearing it would be his knowing I had.

"Uh-huh," he said. "And you made a new friend." He stretched the word out so it sounded like *friiiiiiend.* He was talking about Steph.

"Oh," I said. "Something like that."

Just then there was a call-waiting beep. I looked at my screen. It was a number I didn't recognize. "It's possible he's calling me right now," I said.

"Ew," Xavier said. "*Calling you?* Is he some kind of psychopath?"

"I don't know him well enough to know yet," I said.

The call-waiting beeped again. I sent the call to voice mail.

"Do you *liiiiike* him?" Xavier said. He was trying to sound teasing and fun, but this wasn't even how we usually talked to each other.

I thought he expected me to say something about how I never liked anyone, or how Steph was so not my type or something, but suddenly I didn't want to. *You can practically smell her pussy juicing when she sees you. . . .* Xavier had defended me. I'd heard him defending me. But in that moment, it didn't feel like enough. Maybe nothing would have.

"Who knows," I said. "I had a really good time hanging out with him."

"Wow," Xavier said. "He doesn't seem like he'd be your type."

"What's my type?"

"I don't know. But I mean, that's great. It's great if you had fun. That you had fun."

"Did you?" I said.

"I—" He stopped. "It was all right."

The more we weren't saying, the harder it was to say anything at all. *Spreading like a flow-er.*

"Listen," I said. "I have to go get ready for work."

"Okay," he said.

"Bye," I said. And we hung up.

I got into the shower. I washed my hair, scrubbed my face. I got dressed. All I could think about was Xavier and Ivy, and what I'd decided the night before, how I was going to confront her face-to-face. And whether that was the greatest idea I'd ever had or the very worst one.

I got into my car and drove to the shop. I was seven minutes late, but it didn't matter because no one was there.

I sat alone behind the counter for hours, replaying everything over and over in my head. I was bored. I missed Xavier. I was lonely.

The time moved so slowly. I remembered that Steph had left a voice mail. I decided to listen to it just to have something else to think about for a minute.

"Uh, hey? Sasha? This is Steph. I'm leaving you a voice mail! I was calling you because . . . I wanted to talk to you on the phone. Which is I guess the regular reason people call each other? I don't know. Anyway, call me back. Wait, I just remembered, you put you in my phone as SASHA WHO HATES TALKING ON THE PHONE! Oh crap, sorry. So you can just text. Or whatever. This is Steph." It was sort of a ridiculous message, and yet I weirdly liked the way his voice sounded in the recording, low and husky, and that reminded me of what kissing him had felt like. He had very big hands, and when he had one on my waist and the other on the back of my head, I felt somehow calm and taken care of—I could relax. I don't know why.

Every time we took a break, he'd look at me and shake his head like he could barely believe what was happening. "You're just so . . . ," he'd say. Then he'd shake his head some more. "I'm having the best time with you." And then we'd kiss again and one time he said, "Am I being too gushy? I swear I'm not usually like this . . . like ever, about anyone. Not to sound like a dickhead, but usually roles are reversed, y'know?" And it did kind of make him sound like a dickhead to say it, but also I believed him. Because here's a thing: Steph was very good-looking in a conventional, wholesome kind of way. Far better looking than Xavier, according to most people, probably. Not that it mattered.

I finally called Steph back later that evening when I got home, and he answered after a single ring. He sounded very happy. He invited me to the movies. And aside from being Jake and working at the shop, I didn't have a hell of a lot else going on just then. And it's nice to eat candy in the AC in the dark, and he seemed like a pleasant enough person to go with, so I said yes.

We went to see some dumb comedy, starring this really awful comedian. Steph laughed the whole time, so sweetly and without guile. He kept looking over to see if I was laughing, too. A few times, I faked it to be nice. He held my hand during the movie and kissed me once at the end of the night when he dropped me back at my house. "This was so fun," he said. He was looking at me all lovey and blinky. It was nice to be looked at like that, even though I hadn't done anything to deserve it. "We have to do this again," he said. "Sure," I said, without really meaning it. But the next night, he asked me to go swimming at the swim club his family belonged to, and I said okay. And the night after that, we had cheese fries at a diner. After hanging out three nights in a row, he said, "I know this is really soon, but can I call you my girlfriend?" I said, "How about you call me Sasha?" And he laughed like I was kidding and kissed me on the cheek like we'd just sealed a deal.

August 5, 12:26 a.m.

Ivy: You up?

Jake: Nope. Definitely sleeping. Are you?

Ivy: Sleeping too

Ivy: We've penetrated each other's dreams I guess

Ivy: Yes PENETRATED

Ivy: 😝

Ivy: So that thing about meeting . . . are you still up for it? Or did you get scared like a scared lil baby?

Ivy: Because I just so HAPPENED TO NOTICE you have become awfully quiet on text pal

Jake: Are you sure you don't have a boyfriend? Definitely not the blue haired guy?

Jake: The one in your last pic . . . in the dark by the pool . . .

Ivy: Wow, you're obsessed with him

Jake: You two look pretty cozy. Sorry, don't mean to sound nosy . . . but I've been burned before

Ivy: He's just a friend, and he's gay. And even if he weren't gay, it wouldn't matter because he is just a friend. Okay??

Ivy: Is there anything you're not telling ME?

Jake: There's a lot I'm not telling you . . . heh

Ivy: Tell me what it will be like when we meet

Ivy: If you still want to . . .

Jake: Well, I'll walk in. And I'll be nervous but trying to pretend not to be

Ivy: And I will NOT be nervous at ALL*

Ivy: (*I will be nervous as hell)

Ivy: will you give me a hug right when you see me?

Ivy: Or a kiss?

Jake: it will depend on what you want me to do. What do you want me to do?

Ivy: Are you trying to dirty text me? Is this SEXTING?

Jake: I think so

Ivy: HA. Okay then. I'll do anything you like

Jake: Anything?

Ivy: ANYTHING. Is this how sexting goes?

Jake: I'm not sure we're doing it right

Ivy: Well we're learning

Jake: We can learn together. Go back to the part where you tell me you'd do anything. Would you?

Ivy: Anything . . .

Jake: What if I wanted you to . . .

Ivy: I can see the dots they keep stopping and starting

Jake: I typed something and then deleted it . . .

Ivy: What are you typing that you're so shy to send???

Jake: I am not shy . . . it's just private . . .

Ivy: Your ellipses are very SEXUAL

Jake: Ellipses are the most erotic punctuation

Jake: . . .

Jake: . . .

Ivy: Oh yeah, you hot thing you . . .

Ivy: But what were you typing? For real?

Jake: I'll type it again but not click send . . . we can do a test and see if you're psychic

Ivy: Okay, I'm ready. I'm opening myself up to the POWER of the universe. Your RAW SEXUAL POWER

Jake: Perfect. Okay, I'm about to do it. Starting . . . NOW

Ivy: I'm closing my eyes . . . I see all the dots. Okay and . . . yup, I think I know now what you were asking me to do. ☺

Jake: You do? You got the message?

Ivy: Yup. I got it

Jake: And . . . ?

Ivy: I'm into it. ☺ But really though, I'll do whatever you want . . . including that. Especially that . . . perv

Jake: How do you know me so well already when we haven't even met? ☺

Ivy: Guess it must be fate . . .

Jake: Guess so . . .

Jake: Goodnight Ivy

Ivy: Sweet dreams Jake

Xavier

The morning after Nikolai's party, after that weird phone call with Sasha, Xavier had tried his best to go back to sleep. But there were too many thoughts racing in his head and he didn't know what to do with all of them. So he'd lain there with his eyes closed and his fan blowing straight into his face, waiting and waiting for them to stop. And that's when he got the text from Ivy:

I'm in your driveway. I have food. Please come. I am so, so, so sorry.

Xavier went outside and got into her car, and then there they were with the AC cranked up. Xavier braced himself for what he knew was coming.

Ivy had been wearing a big pair of sunglasses. When she took them off, it looked like she hadn't slept. He hadn't slept much either.

"I am garbage," she said. "I was drunk and way out of line. I am a stupid, horrible idiot. Please forgive me, and forget everything I said. I am awful."

Her eyes had filled up with tears. Xavier's stomach started to hurt, the way it always did when this happened.

"You're not garbage, you're not awful. Please don't say those things. Seriously, it's okay."

He understood what jealousy could do to a person. He understood what drinking could do, too. He knew that Ivy just freaked out sometimes, but part of him was feeling . . . tired. Just a little tired of the whole thing. The tiredness would go away, of course. He had told himself for sure that it would. It was strange, though, to feel anything but love and longing and awe when it came to Ivy. He never had the first time around.

Xavier and Ivy had unwrapped their bagels and cranked the radio. Ivy leaned her head onto his shoulder. Xavier turned and kissed her on the forehead. But it hadn't felt right. It was like he was playing the role of boyfriend on a TV show. Xavier remembered how to do all the things he was supposed to do, but he wasn't sure how to feel. Maybe he hadn't been quite sure how to feel ever since they'd gotten back together.

But as they ate, mostly what he was thinking about was Sasha. The stuff Ivy had said about her had kind of sparked something—that was the problem with words, even if you didn't mean them, once they were out there they *did* things. They did things, just floating around in the air like that. He knew that Sasha wasn't secretly whatever about him, but somehow hearing Ivy say all that had opened up a tiny door in his skull that had maybe been locked shut for a very long time, and behind that door were two words: *what if.*

It's not like it had never occurred to him to think about her in a datey sort of way. He was attracted to girls, and Sasha was a girl. And while Xavier didn't really have a type, in terms of what a girl looked like, if Xavier had to pick one, he might pick strong. And Sasha sure as hell was that. But she was his best friend, in the best-friend box in his brain, and she hadn't been anything else in a very long time.

When they'd first paired up in class, it had occurred to him that Sasha was the sort of person he usually got interested in. But Xavier had had enough with hopeless crushes, and Sasha was someone he *liked* so much just as a human. So he put any other feeling or hint of one so far aside that he basically forgot about it. Xavier liked how sure of herself she was, how funny and smart and strange. And he liked how tough she was, though later he realized that hidden under all that toughness was a person who cared ferociously about anyone lucky enough to be her friend. And he liked that, too.

But what if there were other hidden things that Xavier didn't see?

When they'd finished eating, Ivy turned toward him. She seemed much happier and more awake. She leaned over and took the little glass pipe out of her glove box, and said, "Let's get high and go to the thrift store." But the idea of being high right then, with the sun glaring down on them and his brain all in knots, had seemed very unsettling. So he said, "No thank you," and she shrugged, and said, "Suit yourself," and lit the pipe and filled the car up with smoke, and when she was high and smiley, they drove to the Salvation Army. She tried on 90's prom dresses and bought a floor length glitter one that she said she was going to cut the bottom off of and make into a minidress. And Xavier reminded himself that there were many things about Ivy that he really did adore, and if he didn't feel connected to her every second of every day, that was fine, wasn't it?

But four days after the party, things were still kind of weird. Ivy was trying harder than usual. She texted him in the morning and said they were going out for breakfast, and she was coming to pick him up in ten minutes. Ivy did not believe in diners, as a general rule. She said they always had very good chewing sound acoustics and the sound of people chewing made her want to barf, which was convenient as diner food made her want to barf, too. But when she suggested Kettle 'n' Griddle, his favorite diner in the world, who was he to say no?

Fifteen minutes later, they were in a booth near the back. Ivy wasn't saying much. And Xavier could not help but think about the last time he had been there, six weeks before, with Sasha. She had challenged him to a pancake-eating contest, and Xavier said "To see who can eat the most or who can eat them the fastest?" and she said, "No, the contest is to see who can eat them the *best*," and so they spent the rest of breakfast eating in complicated and glamorous ways, and in the end decided they both had won, since she had come out ahead in the style competition and Xavier won for *flair*. He thought about how he and Sasha always had so much fun there, the two of them, so much fun anywhere.

Then just like that, like he'd summoned her with his mind, Sasha walked in.

She was up at the front register and hadn't yet seen him. A moment later, that guy Steph from the party came up right behind her, slid an arm around her waist, the way a boyfriend would.

It was really strange to see. Sasha didn't *have* relationships. She didn't want them. She made out with people and didn't get attached. It was one of her Things. So then what was going on here? Xavier turned and Ivy was watching them, too. "Hey, Steph!" she called out, too loud. A handful of people turned to look at her. "Hey, Sasha!!" She was suddenly smiling bright, like Sasha and Steph were her very favorite people. They looked up. Steph had a big friendly grin on his big handsome face. "Come sit!" Ivy said.

"Wait, what are you doing?" Xavier said. He had a very bad feeling about this, but it was too late. Steph said something to Sasha, she shrugged, and then a moment later the two of them were right in front of the booth. Ivy hopped out to slide in next to Xavier. Sasha and Steph slid in across from them. And just like that, the four of them were together like it was a double date or something. Sasha gave Xavier a small smile and said, "Hey, buddy," but she didn't look him in the eye.

As they sat there at the diner, Xavier realized that being able to make meaningless small talk in a group is not only an incredible skill, but a gift to the world. And Steph was a master at it. He either didn't notice or didn't care about the strange energy simmering between the other three people at the table as he carried the entire conversation from one topic to the next. Things he brought up included a recent movie he had seen with his favorite comedian in it, the question of why movie candy is so much more expensive than regular candy (because "C'mon! It's the same candy!"), and a description of a funny YouTube video of a monkey. All Xavier could think was that, yes, he is incredibly handsome and good-looking and seemingly full of energy and love for life, but he was *missing* something, some spark. His view of the world was exactly what deodorant ads and car-insurance commercials said it should be. He thought all the normal things and no weird ones, which didn't seem right for Sasha. She deserved someone who *got* her. And Xavier couldn't imagine Steph getting her at all.

Midway through their pancakes and coffees, Steph and Sasha were talking about some summer camp Steph used to go to that was rumored to be haunted, and Ivy leaned close to Xavier and whispered right into his ear, "Steph tried to fuck me once. I didn't do it, though." Then she slid her hand up his shorts and pinched him lightly on the thigh. She left her hand there. Xavier tried to wriggle away.

"The thing is," Steph was saying, "even after they *caught* the squirrel, there were still the same noises. So was it a ghost squirrel? Is *that* who the ghost was?"

"It's weird that you don't hear about animal ghosts more often," Sasha said. Xavier could tell from her tone that she was distracted. "Since there are far more dead animals than dead people in the world."

"Maybe animal ghosts only appear to other—" Xavier started to say, but then Ivy slid her hand all the way up, and she squeezed. Xavier gasped, and not in a good way. He could see Ivy's lips curving into a tiny satisfied smile. Xavier tried to take her hand and move it, but she wouldn't let go. "Animals," Xavier finished. She pressed her leg against his and started swirling her fingers in the way that Xavier usually liked. But Xavier did not like it then. She reached for her coffee with her other hand and raised it slowly to her lips. She was staring at Steph.

"My little brother says he saw a ghost of our dog once," Steph began.

Xavier turned toward Ivy and shook his head slightly. She just smiled. This did not feel sexy or fun. It was wrong and weird, especially considering everything. He looked up and

Sasha caught his eye, then she looked quickly away. And for a horrifying second Xavier wondered if maybe she knew what was going on beneath the table.

"But the thing was, our dog was *alive* at the time. . . ."

Xavier slid across the bench as far away as he could. Finally, Ivy let go.

"But your dog was *alive*?" Ivy said. She leaned forward. "That's so crazy!"

"I know! That's just the thing! Except a few months later, our dog actually got hit by a car. My brother said the dog ghost was time traveling, but I'm like '*Casey, you are high!*'" Steph swallowed a gulp of his juice. "But also we were so sad about our dog that we kind of wanted to believe it, anyway. Sir Barksy was the best guy." He turned toward Sasha. "I wish you'd gotten to meet him. You would've loved the fuzz ball." He smiled at her in this very boyfriendy way. But the weirdest part was the way Sasha smiled back. Like, *Yes, I wish I could meet every pet you've ever had.* A moment later, Steph's phone rang. He grabbed it. "I'm sorry, guys. It's my grandma's birthday and my mom said she'd call me when she got to the nursing home she lives at so . . ." He slid out of the booth. "Hi, Gran-Gran!" he shouted into the phone. And he walked right out the door.

"You guys look cute together," Ivy said. She smiled at Sasha. "Steph's great." Xavier supposed she was trying to be nice then, to make up for what happened at the party maybe. But Xavier felt protective of Sasha. He didn't want Ivy talking to her at all.

"Yeah," Sasha said. "He's a good guy."

The three of them sat there in silence for a moment. "These pancakes are so yummy," Ivy said finally. "Sasha, this is one of your favorite places, right? Xavier said you guys used to come here together a lot."

Sasha looked at her. "Totally my favorite," she said. "Just dee-lish."

A few minutes later, Steph came back to the table. They paid the check and all got ready to leave. When Xavier's and Sasha's eyes met, suddenly he understood something. He wasn't quite sure how he knew, but deep in his gut he was sure of it. At the party, when Ivy had said all that insane stuff about Sasha? Sasha had overheard absolutely everything.

August 6, 1:11 a.m.

Jake: Okay, so here's a question: what are you doing on Thursday?

Jake: Because I think it's time we finally meet.

Ivy: Wait. Are you serious?

Jake: Yes

Ivy: Oh my god

Ivy: let's do it

Jake: Can we meet at 8:30? Things are less terrifying at night

Ivy: You'll be terrified?

Jake: No, I was thinking of you. You'll be terrified. HEH

Ivy: Where should we go?

Jake: There's a diner in your town . . . I just looked it up. Kettle n Griddle. It's 24 hours

Ivy: A diner? Are you sure?

Jake: We can eat pancakes and stare at each other's faces

Jake: We can listen to Finbeeyato and have a two person dance party

Ivy: I am sick of pancakes

Jake: You can get a waffle

Ivy: Thank you

Jake: Ice cream even

Ivy: FANCY MAN

Jake: Nothing but the best for my girl . . .

Ivy: Are you scared?

Jake: I've never been more excited for anything in my life

August 9, 7:49 p.m.

TwistedTree16: Hey, Jake. Change of plans: Let's meet in the woods near my house instead. We can be alone. Cool?

JakeJones1717: Wait . . . what? Why???

TwistedTree16: I texted you a map

JakeJones1717: But what about that Kettle n Griddle place?

TwistedTree16: Fuck the diner

JakeJones1717: Aren't you scared to meet in the woods? I'm a stranger

TwistedTree16: You're not a stranger. And if anyone should be scared it should be you

JakeJones1717: I AM

TwistedTree16: Jake . . . just meet me in the woods. You won't regret it

Sasha

And yet there was a part of me that didn't really believe I would go through with it, not until I found myself getting into my car that Thursday night. And that's when I realized: *Holy fuck, this is actually happening.*

It had been hot all day, the air thick and heavy and still, like the whole world existed inside somebody's mouth. I had sent Xavier a text earlier that afternoon, a final attempt to get him to realize what was going on, but only because I felt I had to. I wrote: I think Ivy is cheating. Steph said Gwen said. Check her phone. He wrote back rumors shmumors ☺. And the truth was, I was glad. I *wanted* to confront her. I was excited to. I was ready.

I didn't put on the stereo as I drove. I didn't sing. I cranked the air conditioner. I was cool and clear. I thought about how I was saving Xavier. I thought about how I was saving myself.

I parked on the side of the road. I got out. The sun was on its way down. I knew after this, everything would be different.

I headed into the woods.

I cannot believe who I have become.

I did not know I was capable of feeling this. And I am so nervous.
I AM SO NERVOUS, I AM SICK.

I know after I meet him, everything will be different.

It's like that dream where you find a door to a new room in your
house, except the door is Jake and the new room is an entirely other
world.

Look, I'm not some idiot, okay?

I know that everyone who falls in love thinks this. I know that love
makes people into dumb dummy idiots who believe they are special.

I know that everyone thinks their love is the REALEST LOVE,
that no one else has ever felt it before as much as they do.

But here is a secret, just a little secret that I know is true. Everyone
thinks it, but me and Jake? We are the only ones who are right.

Sasha

I spotted Ivy through the trees before she saw me. She was sitting on a tire swing. A string of yellow LED bulbs was wrapped around the rope, lighting her up in gold. The air was warm and dim, the sun had just set.

I watched her—twisting in the swing, gently smiling. It had been eighteen days since this all began. Eighteen days and thousands of messages. I imagined what she must be thinking, out here in the woods, waiting for Jake. I imagined the night she thought was in store for her, so different than the one she was going to get.

I took a breath and stepped into the clearing. Ivy turned and looked at me. My body was buzzing with adrenaline. This was it.

For a moment, we just stared at each other.

"Hello, asshole," I said. "Surprise."

She pursed her lips ever so slightly and raised one dark eyebrow.

She didn't understand what was happening. "I'm who you're waiting for," I said. "I'm Jake."

Slowly Ivy's face transformed in that golden light, and she opened her mouth and out came a dirty cackle. "You sick fuck," she said.

"Break up with Xavier or I'll tell him everything," I said.

She shook her head. "Oh, come *on*. You think I didn't know it was you?"

Ivy reached down her shirt, brought out a lighter, flicked it. She lit a thin hand-rolled cigarette. A joint, maybe. She took a long drag and blew out a curl of smoke. She sucked her teeth and stared at me. She was bluffing, wasn't she? Of course she was. My heart was pounding.

She pulled herself out of the swing, joint clenched between her teeth. She walked toward me, slowly smiling.

"Stop lying," I said. "You wrote to me because you thought I was a hot guy who liked you and . . . If you knew it was me, then why did you come here?" I tried to keep my voice calm. I had no idea what to believe.

"For proof," she said. She reached into her pocket and took out her phone. There was a sudden burst of blinding light as she snapped a picture. "So should I upload this right to Instagram or tell Xavier first, do you think?"

I could barely breathe. I pointed to her phone. "Delete that."

Ivy grinned and shook her head. "Nah. I thought he deserved to know the truth about what a fucking psycho you are, and now he finally will."

The blood was hammering in my ears.

And in that moment I realized how incredibly fucking stupid I'd been. I was so desperate for the satisfaction of getting to confront her, that I convinced myself it was a safe bet. I thought Ivy would do whatever I said just to avoid Xavier knowing what she'd written. That she'd be so ashamed and all the power would be mine. And if she protested I could threaten to show her messages to the world, and make her soft squishy core public. But in all the versions of this scene that I'd ever played out in my head, I had never for a second imagined this one.

And maybe she was lying. But maybe she wasn't.

I couldn't be sure of anything anymore.

I started to reach for her phone. She shoved it into her pocket. Then in one swift motion, Ivy grabbed me by the neck of my T-shirt, bunched it up in her fist and yanked me toward her, hard. Our faces were almost touching. Then she pushed me back.

She stuck a foot into the center of the tire and pulled herself up. "Maybe I should just call him right now, and we can all talk about it," she said.

"Delete the picture!" I said. I reached for the swing. The tire was heavy and cold. I started to climb too.

"Oh, you're coming to get me? Maybe it's not just him you're obsessed with. Maybe you're obsessed with both of us, hmm?" She swung her foot forward toward me, her heel colliding with my jaw. My teeth rattled and hot pain shot through the side of my face. I grabbed the rope to steady myself.

The swing jerked. Ivy stumbled. She windmilled her arms, teetering on the edge of the tire.

And then she fell.

She landed on the ground with a sick heavy *thunk*. Her head cracked against the base of the tree.

A shot of adrenaline exploded in my stomach.

Ivy wasn't moving.

I jumped off the swing.

"Ivy." I leaned in. "IVY!?"

I touched her shoulder, gently at first, then harder. I shook her. My heart was pounding so hard. "Oh my God."

Ivy's eyes popped open. "Boo!" The joint was still pinched between her fingers. She stuck it into her mouth and sat up. "Sorry, you're not that lucky," Ivy said. She laughed. "I actually feel sad for you." I could smell alcohol on her breath, sour and sharp. "What did you think would happen out here? That I'd weep and cry and boo-hoo and beggy beg you not to tell?" She paused, took another drag of her joint. She rubbed the back of her head. "Too bad, turns out you're the one who's going to do the begging!"

"You're bluffing," I said.

"Think whatever you want," she said, with a slow grin. "By morning he'll finally know who you really are."

She held her phone out then, and turned it toward me so I could see the picture she'd taken.

And for a moment, everything stopped—there I was, eyes wild, mouth twisted into a snarl, fingers raised to block the light. Seeing myself there on her screen, something inside me flipped.

I looked crazy. Sick, insane.

I looked like a monster.

Maybe I was one.

I stood up, hands shaking. I turned, and I ran. "Aw don't leave now, Peaches!" Ivy shouted after me. But I just kept going.

He'll finally know who you really are.

He'll finally know who you really are.

He'll finally know who you really are.

I had wanted to keep him safe from Ivy. But maybe all along I should have been protecting him from someone else, someone just as messed up, and dangerous—me.

Xavier

Xavier had forgotten what it was like when Ivy disappeared. Forgotten what it was like to have a plan with her and wait, and wait, and wait, have her just not show up, stop returning texts, stop answering her phone. But two weeks and five days after she became his girlfriend again, it all came rushing back.

They were supposed to see a movie, the one Steph had been talking about at the diner, starring that dumb comedian who neither he nor Ivy were even into. The comedian had this signature move thing that he would do after he made a joke. He'd go "Oh oh oh" and hold up one hand, like he was waiting for a high-five. It was supposed to be ironic and not ironic at the same time. A lot of people at school loved him. Ivy thought he was horrendous. "He is obviously a sociopath," Ivy had said. "You can see it in his eyes. I'm not even kidding. He's probably killed people." And then she would do a spot-on imitation of him that was both cutting and hilarious.

Not a lot of people knew that about Ivy, how funny she could be when she wanted. Except she usually didn't bother. "Being funny is mostly a waste of time," Ivy had told him once. "I don't really give a fuck about funny."

But the movie was her idea. She said she was excited to go and hate it.

Only, instead of picking him up at 8:30 the way they'd planned, she just didn't. And she hadn't answered his texts or his calls. And now it was 9:17, and the movie had already started and where was she?

When they were a couple the first time around, she used to do this pretty regularly, just vanish without warning. And he would worry so much, feel absolutely certain something horrible had happened to her. By her third disappearance, he'd understood this was just this *thing* she did—she'd vanish for a day or so, then come back with a fake-sounding excuse, or no excuse at all. But always completely fine. And yet, somehow, when she did it the next time, the same fears always came back. Even though the reasonable part of him *knew* she was safe, some other part of him would think, *but what if this time is different?*

And that's what was happening now.

There was the gnawing in his stomach and pounding in his chest, his itchy fingers checking his phone over and over.

He tried to tell himself it was actually insane to worry. But if nothing bad had happened to her, it meant she was just messing with him. Again. And it seemed impossible she'd be doing that now, considering everything, considering how she mostly seemed to be trying very hard to fix things.

So where did that even leave him?

There was a knock on his bedroom door. "Xavier?" It was his mom.

Xavier jumped. "Come in!"

"I'm getting ready to head to Aunt Kay's for the night," his mom said. Aunt Kay and his uncle had just filed for divorce, so his mom was spending a lot of time there to keep her company. "If you need anything, give me a call, of course. Your dad will be back from his business trip tomorrow afternoon, but I'll probably be home before he is."

"Okay," Xavier said.

"Are you . . ." she started to say. Their eyes met. Xavier knew she probably wanted to ask him what was wrong, but he also knew she wouldn't. "Don't stay up too late," she said instead.

She left, and he was all alone. Xavier wasn't sure what he was supposed to do. It was 9:28 now. His heart nearly exploded when a text came.

He felt bad at how disappointed he was when he saw it was from Sasha.

hows your night going??

Xavier so desperately wished he could tell her the truth. She had always been the person he went to with this stuff the first time around. She was the only person he could ever talk to about it. But Xavier knew he couldn't, not anymore.

Great! Xavier wrote back. He stared at Sasha's text from a few hours before, read it for maybe the fiftieth time. I think Ivy is cheating. Steph said Gwen said. Check her phone. He had written back something flippant, but now her words made his stomach twist and twist. *What if she's right? Maybe* that's *what this is about. . . .*

Xavier sat down on the floor in front of his bed.

He sent another text.

Ivy this is so messed up

And then:

But are you okay?

Xavier thought of all the other times this had happened, how Sasha had always been there to talk him through it. Then later, when the panic subsided, he'd try and backtrack. "The thing is, the *real* Ivy is not the one who does crazy stuff," he'd say. "The real Ivy is the sweet one, the one who is funny and fun, and you'd probably really like her if you got to know her." Sasha would try her best to be supportive, and they'd both pretend not to know that Sasha thought he was crazy for being with Ivy at all. "What if the bad Ivy is the real one, too?" Sasha had asked once. But it wasn't really a question.

Xavier realized, in that moment, that when he finally talked to Ivy—because the reasonable part of him *did* understand that she was absolutely okay—he had to break things off.

He had to shut the door and lock it and cover it with cement and melted steel so strong that even Ivy couldn't kick her way through. Because as long as he was with her, this was always going to happen. As long as he was with her, this would never end.

"Ivy is not my girlfriend anymore," Xavier said out loud. "We are breaking up." But he knew there would be no real relief until he talked to her again.

And who even knew when that would be?

He just had to wait, and wait, and wait.

And there was nothing he could do.

Or was there?

Suddenly, Xavier had an idea. He opened his closet and looked in a shoebox at the back. There was a water bottle inside full of tan liquid. It had been there a while. He didn't remember what it even was. He unscrewed the top and took a long gulp. It burned as it went down. Tequila. He hated tequila.

But he hated this feeling even more.

Xavier made up a little game for himself. He took a swig and checked his phone. Then took another swig and checked it again.

Usually, drinking helped, but maybe his tolerance was too high, or maybe his panic was so strong that just alcohol was not enough to dull it. He needed something more.

And then Xavier remembered the pills. He'd decided to stop using them because they took him right out of his brain and body. The last time he took one was many weeks before, back when his heart was broken. He and Sasha had been drinking and watching a nature movie on his laptop, just like normal, and then all of a sudden it was fifteen hours later and he was waking up at 1:00 p.m. in all of his clothes, with his skull being crushed in a vise, and no recollection of anything that had happened. It was like traveling through time, but terrible because Xavier couldn't shake the feeling that he had maybe done something very bad in the time he had skipped over. And there was no way to go back and fix it.

Only now, being out of his brain and body was exactly what he wanted. It's what he needed, just this final time. And so he opened the pill bottle and swallowed one down. And then he curled up on top of his bed, and took another swig.

Xavier remembered what it was like when Ivy disappeared.

But after that, he remembered nothing else.

Only an idiot is surprised by THE BAD THINGS

Only an idiot has HOPE

THAT SOFT SMALL ANIMAL NEXT TO YOUR BED

IT IS WAITING FOR YOU TO FALL ASLEEP

SO IT CAN TEAR INTO YOUR CHEST

AND DEVOUR YOUR HEART

I should NOT have been surprised

I should not have been SURPRISED

I SHOULD NOT HAVE BEEN SURPRISED

So why the fuck am I?

And what am I going to do now?

Sasha

When I got home, I erased as much as I could. I smashed the phone I had used to text with. I deleted Jake's Instagram account and closed down the email address I'd used to make the Instagram, as though that would somehow change anything at all.

All the while, I replayed the night over and over in my head. And the weeks leading up to it. My thoughts got louder and louder and bigger and bigger until they filled up all the space and the house was full of them and they were shaking the goddamn walls. WHAT HAVE YOU DONE, YOU CRAZY FUCK?

I texted Xavier, asked how his night was going, to see how he'd respond. He replied, Great! He didn't know yet.

But he would soon enough.

And when he found out—how would I even begin to explain

it? There was no way I'd be able to convince him that I had had good reasons for all of it, because even I wasn't sure what was true anymore. I doubted everything I thought I knew except for this: I loved Xavier more than anyone in the world. And I would not be able to bear losing him from my life. But I was almost certainly going to. It was what I deserved, and my own goddamned fault.

I did not sleep that night, just watched the hours tick by. I checked Ivy's Instagram again and again, but at 4:00 a.m. the picture wasn't up yet. And I hadn't heard from Xavier either.

I tried to figure out what this might mean. Did it mean she must have been bluffing after all? The more I thought about it, the more I convinced myself. I had started to believe Ivy in the woods because she was a good liar. But I had seen everything she'd written to Jake. And those messages were way too personal to be any kind of trick. She knew it, and I knew it, and she knew Xavier would know it if he ever saw them. I'd started to believe her in the woods because I'd panicked. But I understood the truth now.

She'd never tell him what had happened. And if I didn't either, he'd never know.

At first this realization felt like a relief. But only at first. Because here was the thing: somehow, after everything, keeping this secret no longer felt like an option. Xavier deserved to know what kind of person Ivy really was. He deserved to know what kind of person I really was, too.

By the time the sun came up, I understood what I had to do—regardless of what Ivy was planning, I had to tell him the truth.

I forced myself to wait until 8:30 before I texted him. Can I come over? I need to talk to you. I figured he wouldn't be awake yet, but a few seconds later, I got a reply. Just one word: yes

And a second after that, come now.

That's when I realized that he probably already knew.

Xavier was waiting for me on the steps in front of his house.

I parked and got out, walked toward him. I felt myself starting to sweat. Xavier looked worse than I'd ever seen him, worse even than when Ivy had first dumped him—sweaty, bloodshot eyes half open.

"Xavier," I said. "I . . ." I was so sorry, so, so very sorry. How had I let things go this far?

He took a breath.

"I can't believe it," he said. "But I guess I'm a dummy for not believing it. Because I should have known." He tried to smile but couldn't. It looked like it hurt, like his face was broken. Like his whole body was broken.

"I know," I said. "I'm so sorry I . . ."

"She did it again," Xavier said. He looked up at me. Our eyes met. He quickly looked away. He shook his head. "So it's done now. It has to be done now."

What was he talking about? "What happened?"

"You were so right about everything," he said. He sounded blank and far away. "I really thought it was going to be different this time. I'm so sorry I didn't listen to you. I mean, for my sake, but for yours, too." He shook his head. "I'm so embarrassed that I'm making you listen to this again."

"You never have to be embarrassed," I said. "Not in front of me. Not about anything." And then. "There is literally nothing you could do that would change my opinion about you." *Or make me stop loving you*, I added silently. How I desperately wanted the reverse to be true.

Xavier tried to smile again. "You really are the best friend in the entire world. What would I ever do without you?"

You'd be better off. I almost started to cry then. But I held it in. I held it in for Xavier.

"What did she do?" I said. "What happened?"

"That vanishing thing," he said.

He stared down at his feet. "We had plans last night, but she never showed up or texted me back. Just like she used to before. . . ." His voice cracked. He clenched his jaw. "I waited and waited, and I felt so insane and so terrible and so stupid. I drank a bunch . . . I took some of those dumb pills from before. At some point I passed out, I guess . . . I don't even remember. I woke up this morning wearing all my clothes, my shoes even, and . . ." He paused, then took a slow shaky breath. "I really didn't think it was possible that it would happen again. Which is so stupid. Because of course it would and . . . and . . . your text, I guess she's cheating, now? I guess it doesn't matter at this point. I know you're not the I-told-you-so type, but you can say it now if you want to."

He looked out at the road, then closed his eyes.

"I don't," I said.

"I am done with her," he said. "I have to be. Last night was hell. But at least I know where I stand now. I was even worried about her, if you can believe that. Which was idiotic! Obviously!!"

Xavier had no idea why she had vanished, but I did: Ivy was hiding because she assumed I'd told Xavier what had happened. And that proved for sure she hadn't known I was Jake.

She wouldn't be hiding if she weren't guilty. Of that I was certain.

So now what? Maybe she would just keep on hiding forever. She would never contact him. And he wouldn't contact her either. And with Ivy gone, Xavier wouldn't ever have to know how it all had come about. I felt hope blooming inside me, hope I did not deserve to feel.

But *I* had to tell him the truth, didn't I?

That was what I'd decided. . . .

"I'm so lucky I have you," Xavier said. He smiled at me. His eyes looked strange, like they did not quite belong to him. "I seriously do not know what I would do without you. I truly don't." I felt my brain desperately scrambling for a way out. Maybe it would be better for *him* not to know what I'd done.

Maybe he shouldn't have to be burdened with the knowledge of how awful his best friend had been. And I could become a better person after this. It would be okay not to confess if I just became the person he thought I already was.

"Maybe we can get breakfast now?" Xavier said. "I mean, if you don't have other plans? I feel like crap. Maybe food would help?"

"Yeah," I said. "That would be good. I don't have to work until noon."

He stood up. We walked.

"What did you want to talk to me about?" Xavier asked.

"Nothing important," I said. "I—I've missed you lately."

"I've missed you, too," he said. And he smiled the best he could, and in that moment, it was enough.

My insides uncoiled. Despite all that had happened and all that I'd done, it seemed that somehow, against all odds, everything was going to be okay. Everything would be just fine.

At least that's what I told myself.

Sasha

We went to the diner and ate like it was our last meal on earth. Egg sandwiches and pancakes and a side of sausage and a side of bacon and a Belgium waffle with strawberries and ice cream. "We are *monsters*," Xavier said. And we just kept eating and eating. We growled like beasts, our faces slick with grease and sticky with syrup.

For the first time in a very long time, things between us seemed almost back to normal. Except I never once looked him in the eye. I felt like I couldn't—I didn't deserve to. And if Xavier noticed, he didn't let on.

At the end of the meal, we got a chocolate milkshake to go, mostly as a joke. We knew there was no chance we'd have more than a sip. I drove Xavier back home. In the car, he was quiet again, and he had that same blank look on his face from before.

I went to work after dropping him off. It was a slow day. A

guy copied flyers for his garage sale. A woman came to find out the price of getting a laptop case with her dog printed on it. A couple of kids stopped by and used the Internet.

Mostly I sat behind the counter and tried to keep myself awake, tried to keep myself from thinking too much. Just after four, I spotted Xavier through the big front windows. I felt a rush of joy. It had been a long time since he'd come to visit me at work. But when he got inside I saw his face. He looked even worse than before.

Now he knows for real, I thought. My entire body started to sweat.

He thrust his phone forward. There was a message thread on the screen.

It was a conversation between him and Gwen.

Gwen 3:46: Hey, have you heard from Ivy lately? She hasn't texted me back since yesterday afternoon and I know she had plans with you and I'm getting worried

Xavier 3:46: I haven't heard from her either

Gwen 3:47: You had plans though, right . . .

Xavier 3:47: She didn't show up

Xavier watched me with bloodshot eyes. "What if something actually *did* happen to her? I mean, I get her vanishing on me, but on her best friend?"

I shook my head. "You *know* this is a thing she does," I said. "She's totally fine." But what I was thinking was that she isn't fine, she's freaking out because of what she did and hiding from *everyone* now. And some tiny fucked-up part of me was happy to know that. But I didn't want Xavier to worry. "I promise you, she is absolutely okay and there is nothing to be anxious about."

"I don't know." Xavier looked down. "I know that what you're saying is reasonable, but I just have a really bad feeling that something terrible has happened. . . ."

The shop was empty except for the two of us.

"That's called being hungover," I said. "Remember all the other times she did this? If she was someone else, or hadn't done this a million times already, sure, we'd be concerned now. But she is who she is and she does what she does. That is the only thing going on here."

He nodded at me. "You're right," he said. "I mean, I know you are. Of course you are."

I asked him if he wanted to stay and hang out. "We can print our faces onto stickers and stick them on everything, like we used to," I offered. But he said no thank you, he probably needed to go lie down, because he really was not feeling so great. And then he left. I watched as he walked out the door.

I checked Ivy's Instagram, but still there was nothing new.

It didn't matter. Ivy was fine, obviously. She was clearly freaking out and hiding. Or, hell, maybe she was off with another guy already and not even worrying about any of this.

I tried to stop thinking about it after that, tried to stop thinking about Ivy at all.

A man came in with baby announcements to print.

A lady and her daughter wanted to know if we could print customized softballs.

A couple in their early twenties asked about getting a photo shrunk down small enough to fit inside a locket. One of the women held up the necklace, a big pewter oval on a thick chain. "It's an antique," she said. "An anniversary present." She smiled and waited for me to respond. When I didn't, she shrugged. "You can shrink a photo, right? How much will it cost?"

But I wasn't listening anymore. I reached up and clasped my neck. The locket. My locket. The one my grandmother gave me, the one I wore every day. The one I never took off. It was gone.

I closed my eyes. I remembered the feeling of Ivy's hand on my chest, fist grabbing the neck of my shirt, pulling me toward her. Suddenly, I knew exactly where it was.

I looked up at the two women. "I'm sorry," I said. "But we're closed."

"Your sign says you don't close until five. We are literally inside the store talking to you. So you are obviously open."

I felt the tears welling up. "Oh shit," the one with the necklace said. She leaned in close to her girlfriend and whispered something. Then she grabbed her hand and pulled her toward the door.

And I headed back to the woods.

I know that the universe does not give a crap about what we do. There is no order, no such thing as fair—*nobody* gets what they deserve. But as I was making my way back to that spot between the trees, I could not help but wonder if perhaps the universe took my grandmother's necklace because I did not deserve to have it. Not after everything I'd done.

As I walked toward the woods, I forced myself to think about my grandmother, even though I usually didn't because it made my chest ache. I forced myself as if it was punishment. The last year of her life she was like a fire going out, the person I knew only appearing in brief flickering sparks. And there were fewer and fewer of them, until one day there was nothing left at all but a wisp of smoke, and then she was gone. My grandmother gave me the necklace after she was already in the nursing home during a rare lucid moment. She managed to get the necklace off with shaking hands and dropped it into my lap. I put it on my own neck, and it had been there ever since. Until now.

Going back to those woods was my only hope of finding it. I walked through the trees. I thought about my grandmother and how much I missed her. I thought and I walked far, far away from everything. How strange that less than twenty-four hours before, I had been on my way to the same place in these same woods. How different I had felt back then.

I stepped between the two biggest trees into the small clearing.

When I first saw the body, my brain could not process it.

Xavier and I had taken mushrooms together once. I was

full of vibrating terror, felt like my skin was shrinking and that my skeleton would burst through and escape. I had thrown up, right onto the ground, saw little tadpoles swimming in it. Saw skull patterns in the sky, furious faces in the grass. Things that weren't real.

Maybe this is like that, I thought.

Maybe someone had slipped me something, or maybe I was going crazy.

I blinked and shook my head and stopped breathing and started again, but no matter what I did, it was there. The body was still there.

I saw toes. Small and round, chipped silver polish on the nails. An ankle with a silver chain around it, a mosquito bite, a shaving cut. Thin calves, wiry dancer's thighs. Frayed cut-off shorts. An oversize gray hoodie, hands sticking out the bottom of the sleeves. Dark hair blending in with the dirt. A tiny pointed chin. Big eyes, wide open.

Who takes a nap with their eyes open? Who takes a nap on the ground in the dirt? With dirt and leaves in their hair and flies buzzing around, landing on their face, and they are not swatting them away?

Ivy was fucking with me.

"Hey!" I said. My head was underwater.

I crouched down. "Ivy!" She was very good at not blinking. You need to blink, because eyes are wet balls rolling around in your skull, but there she was, staring and staring and not blinking at all. I hated her so much for doing this now. For lying there in the woods and seeming so convincingly like just a body. Like just a body that was not moving.

So very, very convincingly dead, so dead that she was not breathing or blinking, and her skin was not quite the right color, and her lips were so very dry—how the fuck? Howthefuckwasshedoingthis?

"How the fuck are you doing this?"

But Ivy didn't answer.

I stood up and stumbled back.

Ivy was dead in the woods?

Is that what this meant? Is that what finding Ivy lying on the ground in the woods not moving or breathing meant?

She was so very small. I stared at her fingers, at her little tapered fingers, fingernails bitten down to the quick.

I closed my eyes and asked my brain for some answers. Nothing made sense at all. I only knew one thing: What seemed to be in front of me was not possible. What I was looking at had not happened and this was not possible. How could this possibly be?

Ivy's fall.

I remembered then the sickening *thunk* of her skull against the tree. The way she looked as she lay on the ground. I remembered how shocked and terrified I felt. I remembered her sitting up and laughing at me because she was fine.

And I suddenly understood that she had not actually been fine at all.

People hit their heads, seem okay as their brains silently swell up and kill them in their sleep. Their brains bleed and bleed inside their skulls, and nobody knows it until their brains drown and they are gone. It happens every day. It had happened to Ivy.

My entire body was tingling.

Ivy was dead on the ground.

She was dead on the ground because I grabbed that rope.

And because, before that, I had tricked her for weeks, lured her out into the woods. Lured her here and threatened her and grabbed onto that rope.

And she fell backward and hit her head.

I looked down at Ivy's toes. At my shoes. I looked at the trees, Ivy's fingers, at the sky. I tried to remember anything else that had ever happened before this moment.

What did I need to do? Call an ambulance? Call the police?

I stood there, heart beating so hard I could feel it in my teeth. I was out there in the woods, alone with Ivy's body. And the world was silent and still.

And then . . . there was music. That song Ivy had danced to at the party.

For one brief shimmering moment, I had hope. I teetered on the crystal-clear edge of it: if there was music playing now, maybe this *wasn't* actually real. Not real in the way I had thought at first. This was a setup, a prank. This wasn't really Ivy's body, but a great replacement. A prop. Nothing that happened in movies was real, but it all looked real. Just like how Jake seemed to be real. But I'd made him up. The truth hardly even mattered. The world could make you believe anything at all.

How had this happened? It hadn't.

As long as the music played, I could believe that it hadn't.

But the music stopped. I turned around and looked to see who was watching me, who was out there in the woods playing that music. I couldn't see anyone. And when the music started again, I was still alone.

Except for Ivy.

And this was real.

And that music was her phone, ringing halfway out of her pocket. A picture of Xavier was flashing on the screen.

Sorry, Ivy can't come to the phone right now.

It started ringing again, ringing so loud someone was going to hear it and come find me standing over Ivy in the woods. Me alive and Ivy dead. I had to make the ringing stop while I figured out what to do next. I reached down, shuddered when I touched it. Ivy's phone. The dead girl's phone. The very same kind as mine. But there was no time for thinking, no time for planning.

I could not be there, standing over her in the woods, me alive while Ivy was dead.

But my limbs knew what to do and they were doing it

without me. My hand held the phone, I rejected the call. The music stopped. My breath was stuck. My heart was beating in my ears. And then somehow Ivy's phone was in my pocket and my feet were pounding against the earth, pounding against the dirt and the grass and the leaves, taking me away as fast as I could go.

Xavier

The hangover was not a regular one. Xavier felt sick and insane. Back at home, he got into bed, pulled the covers up over his head. He lay there and waited while his brain tried to escape his skull.

He called Ivy. He called her again. The third time the phone rang only a few times before it went to voice mail. Had she rejected the call? Or was that the normal amount of rings?

Xavier wanted so desperately to believe that Sasha was right, that Ivy was fine. That he was just hungover. But somewhere deep in his gut, Xavier knew this was different. Somewhere deep in his gut, Xavier knew nothing would ever be okay again.

Xavier's mom got back from her night away. She looked worried. Did Xavier maybe need to make another appointment with Dr. Carol? No thank you, Xavier said. Then Xavier went to the bathroom and threw up as quietly as possible.

You're never going to talk to Ivy ever again, his brain said. Xavier didn't even know why he thought that.

Xavier lay on his floor and stared at the ceiling. His whole body hurt, like he'd been in a fight.

He closed his eyes. He tried to think of anything but how scared he was and how sick he was. He tried to slow his breathing, to quiet his heart.

It wasn't working, it wasn't working, it wasn't working.

But then, finally, the text came.

A text from Ivy.

At first, he didn't care what the words of the text even *were*, he could barely focus his eyes, anyway. But just the fact of hearing from her at all was enough, was all he wanted. Then, hands shaking, he finally read what she'd sent.

I don't want to do this anymore. It was a mistake to try again. Don't bother texting back. Srry

He read it again.

And again.

He closed his eyes and lay back on the floor again to stop the room from turning over.

It seemed completely impossible that Xavier had received that message at all. That after everything, *this* is how it would end. Again. It made no sense. Which is why it made perfect sense—because that was her, that was Ivy. She'd always surprise you.

Xavier braced himself, waited for the sadness to come. Even though he'd decided he was done with her, there's a difference between deciding and having it decided for you. Xavier waited for the familiar dark pit to beckon. But instead, his brain gave him a gift, a thought so clear and reasonable, it felt like it was coming from someone else's head—Xavier didn't have to try and figure any of this out.

He could just stop.

He could just let her go.

Goodbye, Ivy.

He whispered it out loud.

And then, as though those words were magic, the spell that had bound him to her since the moment he first saw her watching him run up that snowy hill was finally broken.

He felt a rush of joy, even through the hangover. A rush of dizzying relief. He was so ready to be finished with all of this, with this entire part of his life, to make everything that had ever happened with Ivy a distant memory. He texted his best friend:

Can we please go out and do something fun tonight? Sloe Joe's??? This whole Ivy nightmare is finally done. I am free!!

Sasha

I gave myself an hour. One hour to tell Xavier the truth—not the truth of what I'd done, but the truth of how I felt. I had to get it out, now, while I still could. Then, when I was finished, I would drive myself to the woods. I would go back to Ivy's body. I would call the police and tell them everything. And they would come and get her. Come and get both of us.

"Dance like the room is full of spiders!" Xavier was bopping next to me. He wiggled his fingers near his face.

Three weeks earlier, I had stood in the same spot at Sloe Joe's and danced with Xavier on the night of his birthday. Now we were back, but there was a thick layer of cotton between me and the world. I wasn't really here. I wasn't anywhere.

How was any of this even possible?

"Dance like your hands have become spiders, actually. But

you're cool with it!" Xavier did spider fingers on my shoulder, then took my hand, shook it around. I closed my eyes, gritted my teeth. I held on tight.

I imagined what Xavier would think later when he looked back at this night. When he finally knew what had happened, and understood that I had known all along. He would remember me drinking, and dancing, holding his hand.

He would remember the text message he got from Ivy and know that I was the one who had sent it. I shivered in the heat in the dark.

What the fuck had I been thinking? Even I could barely explain it. I was there in the woods, outside my body, and nothing felt real. It still didn't. But I knew how worried he was, how terrible it was for him to be waiting and waiting for that text. And I realized then that he'd be waiting forever now. . . .

I had just wanted to give him a moment of relief. A moment of relief before there was none.

I watched him. He caught me staring and waggled his tongue through his teeth. He was different than I'd seen him in a very long while, smiling, chugging rum from a bottle he'd brought in his bag. He seemed so happy.

He leaned in close, his mouth against my ear. "I can't believe I spent so long being so obsessed," Xavier called out over the music. "I can't believe I spent *months* like that. It's crazy to think this time yesterday I was going out of my mind. So out of my mind I had to take myself *completely* out of my mind. I *blacked out*. I was not even *on this planet*. And now here I am with you, and everything . . ."

Xavier was looking me straight in the eye. He pulled me toward him. His skin was hot, like he was on fire. ". . . and everything feels . . ." He leaned in. Something was happening. Something I had waited so very, very long for. And wanted so very, very badly.

I could barely breathe.

I closed my eyes. And when I opened them, there was his sweet face, flushed from alcohol and dancing, lips slightly apart. He leaned in closer, closer still.

But I couldn't do this.

I stepped back.

"Whatever happens next," I told him, "just know that . . ."—*I love you*—". . . I'm so, so sorry."

And I forced myself to look away, because I could not bear to see his eyes, how they'd change or how they wouldn't. I could not bear to see whatever would happen next on his face, because whatever he might think he meant now . . . he sure as hell wouldn't mean it tomorrow.

So I turned and I tried to run. He caught me by the wrist. His hand was strong. And he was holding me so tight. For a moment, I actually couldn't get away.

"What's going on?" he said. He sounded desperate. "Talk to me."

But I didn't turn back even to look at him, I just shook my

head. "Let me go." I yanked my arm again. He held on for a moment longer and then he released me.

"Wait!" he called after me. "Please!"

I was running then, the blood rushing in my ears. When I got to the door, I turned back one last time. I saw his face and it cracked me clean through, he looked so hurt and confused. And so, so scared.

I ran all the way back to the train. I wondered what he could possibly be thinking, what he could possibly be imagining, and I knew, no matter what it was, the truth was so much worse.

Xavier

Xavier stood in the center of the dance floor, noise and lights all around him, but all he could see was the expression on Sasha's face as she pulled away. All he could hear was her voice: *Let me go.*

She had looked at him like he was crazy. What if she was right?

Xavier was more confused than he had ever been. He replayed everything that had led up to this, trying to figure it out.

It seemed insane to him that less than twenty-four hours before, he'd been full of panic about *Ivy*. How was that even possible? Now that he was free of her, it felt like it had all happened a million years ago.

He'd been so excited to see Sasha tonight. *That* was the main thing on his mind. It had gotten awfully strange between them, and he had missed her very much, maybe more than he even realized. He was ready to be done with the Ivy part of his life, to be back to normal. Or better than normal.

But the night had started off a little funny—Sasha was in a mood he couldn't quite figure out. They met up at the train station, and she seemed very far away. When he asked her about it, she just said she was fine, except she wasn't talking much. He wondered if she was mad at him. He wondered if he should mention what had happened at Nikolai's party and apologize. But he'd already subjected her to more than enough drama, hadn't he? He owed her a night of simple fun without him bringing anything else into it. So he took out his rum and they started to drink.

And that's when things changed. They got to Sloe Joe's. They kept drinking. And he felt this overwhelming rush of joy spreading through his whole body. It was summer, and he was young and free and out with his favorite person, and they had the whole night ahead of them. They danced, got closer and closer.

And it had started to seem like maybe something was happening between them. He thought he wanted it to and maybe she did too and maybe they'd been taking baby steps toward it for a while.

Then all of a sudden she was pulling away. *Let me go.* He thought about the horrified expression on her face and the look in her eyes, right before she turned and ran.

What the hell had he done?

Sasha

Back in the woods again.

Right foot, left foot, right foot, left foot.

It was still early. The setting sun poured pink through the trees. And there was Ivy on the ground. It seemed impossible, but there she was. I didn't let myself look at her face, not yet. I had to find my necklace first. I'd find my necklace and then call the police. I wondered where they'd send me when they got us, if I'd be allowed to have a necklace there.

I searched among the bugs and dirt and sticks and leaves. There it was, right near the base of the tree. I reached down to the soft earth and grabbed the locket, held it tight.

I forced myself to look at Ivy's face then. There was a tingling behind my eyes, and I knew I was about to lose it—I was about to fall apart entirely. I wanted to cover her in a blanket, like she was just asleep. I wanted so desperately to wake her up.

"I'm sorry," I said. I stared at her tiny pointed chin, her wide mouth, that space between her two front teeth. "I'm so sorry." I leaned in.

Then I gasped. Not because of what I'd done, but because of what I saw. Marks around Ivy's neck.

They were half obscured by her bunched-up sweatshirt, but I could see them now, peeking up over the top of her collar. I pushed the thick fabric out of the way, and there were more— the red and purple dots mottling her skin, arranged in clusters in a thick band around her neck, dark against light, like a reverse Milky Way.

What the fuck is this?

But I knew—suddenly and for certain.

These were choke marks.

I closed my eyes.

But I had never touched her neck.

All at once, the thoughts clicked into place.

Ivy was dead.

But I hadn't killed her.

She was choked to death.

I raised my hand to my throat.

I had no idea how to feel.

What to think.

What to do.

Someone had killed her.

Who?

Why?

All I knew was the when and the how. Sometime between when I left her last night and before I saw her this afternoon, hands had been around her throat, squeezing tight, squeezing until there was nothing left.

I was dizzy and sick.

I looked at her face, her neck, her legs, her arms, at her hands, curled into the sleeves of her sweatshirt and I noticed something else. I leaned in close. Blue strands. There were delicate light blue strands like threads but thinner, tangled between her fingers, catching the light. Tangled between her fingers like she'd grabbed them and yanked them as she desperately gasped for air through her closed throat and did not find any.

Blue strands.

Xavier's hair.

I remembered what Xavier had said, how he had no recollection of the night before. He'd taken pills and drank and blacked out. He said he felt like maybe he'd done something terrible that he couldn't remember.

Time stopped. And in the space between seconds, my brain sped up and I understood two things:

One—something had happened between Xavier and Ivy, and now she was dead with his hair in her hands. And he had no recollection of any of it, of being with her at all. I *knew* he didn't, he wasn't making that up. I'd seen his face that morning, the panic, the fear. It was genuine and real.

And two—I could not call the police, not anymore.

Sweet, gentle Xavier. Sweet Xavier who was sensitive and kind and caring, would never knowingly hurt anyone ever. And if he did, even by accident, the very thought would destroy him. Whatever had gone on out here, there was no chance that Xavier had been aware of it, or had done it on purpose. Whatever had gone on, whatever he did, he didn't remember. He never would.

And I couldn't let him try.

It was my fault. I had made this terrible, awful mess. And now I had to clean it up.

What happens when the unimaginable is right in front of you? What happens when you have to make a decision you can't possibly make?

The world cleaves in two. And suddenly you are outside yourself watching, watching, watching to see what you do.

We are, all of us, stronger than we realize. Maybe it is good to know, but you'd trade it all for never having had to find out. Pray you never find out how strong you are. Pray you never find out how much you can carry, how much you can bear, how many secrets you can keep.

And where you can hide them.

Xavier

Xavier woke up with the sun. Before he even opened his eyes, he was thinking about Sasha. And what had happened the night before.

He felt a twisting in his stomach, and he pressed his face into his pillow. Oh Lordy, he sure had messed things up. But maybe he could fix it.

He had an idea.

His father was in the kitchen getting ready to leave for work. Xavier asked him to drop him in town on the way.

Fifteen minutes later Xavier stood at the counter of the old-fashioned bakery. He bought seven cinnamon sugar donuts, the kind they were known for that always sold out. Then he walked to her house. "I have those seven cinnamon sugar donuts you asked for," he planned to say. Seven was the funniest number of something to get to give a person. And

things had gotten so strange between them, only a joke could
fix it. Unless showing up at her house would make things
weirder.

Would it?

He suddenly wondered if maybe he should turn around,
maybe he should make his way back home. But by then he
was at her house and saw that she was already outside. For a
moment it felt like magic.

"Fancy meeting you out here!" he said. "And it's a really
lucky thing actually because I have your . . ." He held the bag
of donuts out in front of him. The grease had soaked through
the paper.

But when she looked up and saw him, she did not smile.
Xavier felt like he was sinking. His mouth opened and fumbled
for words he had not planned out because he was not yet even
sure what they should be. He lowered the bag of donuts to his
side.

"About last night," he said. "I'm really sorry that . . ." What
was he trying to tell her?

"Seriously, don't worry about it," Sasha said quickly. "There's
nothing to apologize for."

"But I—"

Sasha shook her head, just shook it and held up her hand.
And that's when Xavier noticed the tent and the duffel bag sitting on the ground next to her car.

"Running away from home?" He was trying to make a joke,

to sound casual, but no part of him felt casual. His heart was pounding.

"I have to go," she said. "On a trip." Since when did Sasha go on last-minute trips without even telling him?

He was struck with the terrible fear that his joke was not far off. She was running away. She was leaving because of him, because of what had almost happened between them. She was leaving and never coming back.

Or maybe, he realized, it wasn't even about him at all.

"With who?" he said. But he thought maybe he already knew the answer, and it made him feel sort of sick. "Who are you going on the trip with?"

"No one," she said.

"Really?" He felt a moment of crushing relief. "How come you're going?"

"I just need to go somewhere," she said. "My mom and Marc are out of town again and I called in at the shop and I ..."

"Can I come?" His voice cracked. It was suddenly very, very important to him that she not get into the car and drive away. That she not get into the car and drive away without him.

She shook her head. "That's not a good idea."

"Why not? Is it because of that time I ..." He was trying to think of something funny to say, but then they locked eyes. And he stopped. Hers were completely flat, like she wasn't even in there behind them. Something was going on, and he could not begin to guess what it was. But he knew one thing for sure:

He couldn't leave her to deal with this alone. She'd taken care of him for weeks and weeks, done her best to protect him, to keep him sane. And now it was his turn.

"*Please,*" he said. "Sasha, I know it's been . . . a lot has happened lately. But I need to come with you." She was looking at him, slowly shaking her head. "Whatever it is that's going on, you don't have to tell me. I won't even ask about it, I swear. I'll just sit in the car. I'll be like one of those mannequins people use to ride in the carpool lane. We can ride in the carpool lane!"

"Nothing's going on," she said. But her voice sounded wrong, and he didn't believe it.

"Good," he said. "Great, I'm so glad to hear it." And then he had an idea that was either funny or dumb, but he was going to risk it. He walked over to her car. He opened the door. He got in the passenger seat and sat down. He shut the door and rolled down the window. He leaned the seat back until he was practically lying down. "So when do we leave?" he shouted. "Don't worry, I already packed our donuts!"

Sasha was silent. He sat up. She was still staring at him, her eyes were very shiny. She was starting to soften, he could see it. "I'm not getting out of the car, so either I'm coming with you, or you're gonna have to pick me up and drag me out."

"Xavier," she said.

"Sasha," he said. "Can you pick up a whole human being? A whole human being in addition to an entire bag of seven donuts? I mean, I know you are very strong, but . . ." Xavier stopped, satisfied. Because her face was changing. Was she smiling? Well, no. But she didn't look the same as before, at least.

"You don't even know where I'm going."

"I don't care," Xavier said. "I just want to come. Hang out with my best friend, who I have really missed." His friend who obviously needed his help even though she wasn't going to ask for it.

He leaned halfway out the window, out there with the chirping birds and the blue sky. Somewhere nearby someone had started up a lawn mower.

"So where are we going, anyway?" he said. "Georgia? Canada? To the Moon?"

"South," she said. "I don't know how long it will take." She paused. "What would you tell your parents?"

Xavier knew then that she was going to let him come, and his insides started lifting. "That I'm home but have taken a vow of silence and also a vow of invisibility, so they won't be able to hear or see me?"

"I'm serious," Sasha said.

Xavier thought for a moment. "I'll tell them I'm with you. I'll say I broke up with Ivy and that we're on a trip with your mom and her boyfriend. My mom will be so glad that I'm not stuck in bed this time, and my dad honestly probably won't even notice." Xavier paused. "Please. Please. Please. I'm literally not letting you leave without me so you might as well say yes and save us some time."

When their eyes met, he felt like she was telling him something in a language he couldn't understand. All he knew was that he cared about her more than anyone in the world, and he very, very much didn't want her to drive off without him. He got out of the car then. He picked up the tent and started carrying it around toward the trunk. "I'll help," he said.

"No!" Sasha shouted. "I mean, give that to me. I have . . ." She looked at him. "A whole packing system."

"Since when?" he asked. He was smiling.

"Call your mother," she said. "If you're coming, call her."

So he did. He called his mother and told her they were going on a trip together. And she was happy, just like he knew she'd be.

Xavier got into the car. Sasha already had the motor running.

He gave himself permission to stop thinking. There is a luxury in giving up control, in handing everything over to someone else. Someone who you trust more than anyone in the world. Someone who you know will always take care of you, and you of them. He realized in that moment there was only one person on earth who he had ever felt like that about. And she was right beside him.

"It's like we'd always planned," he said. He got in the car. "Two outlaws on the run." He held up a set of finger guns and shot them high into the sky. "Pew pew!"

"But one rule," she said. "No phones. Take it out and put it back inside." She was playing their game then, the one where she told him what to do. He knew it was because of Ivy— Sasha was worried he'd be tempted to get in touch with her. He wanted to say, *So far as I'm concerned, she might as well be dead*, but he didn't. To refer to her at all would give her power, would put her in the car with them. And he just did not want her there, or anywhere, anymore.

He took his phone out of his pocket. "I'll put it inside," he said. And she nodded. On the way he texted his mom, told her they'd probably be out of range so if she texted or called he wouldn't get it, and she shouldn't worry.

He left the phone in Sasha's room, came back outside, gave her a thumbs-up.

He got into the car. He was glad not to have his phone, he realized, to have nothing connecting him to the world, nothing connecting him to anything but Sasha. He had a flash of good feeling like maybe all the bad things were behind him and there were only good things up ahead now.

He reached out then without even thinking, without even meaning to, and took Sasha's hand. He squeezed it. Her face flushed. She opened her eyes wide. She squeezed his hand back.

"Let's go," she said.

"Road trip!" he said.

She turned the key.

The engine started.

They went.

Part 2

Sasha

People try so hard to figure out how to pretend, but it's easy, really. The simple secret is to trick yourself first, be the thing you're pretending you are. Be the person who believes the lie you need to tell. You are a character in a movie or a play doing the things you need to do, believing the thing you need to believe. You are outside yourself now. It helps if you haven't slept in a very long time and nothing feels real, anyway.

Inhale, close your eyes. Exhale, float away. The old you is gone, and the other you is all that is left. You know what you need to do. Let your pulse pound with it. Taste the salt of it on the tip of your tongue, burn your lips with it.

Swallow it down.

Here is what you knew, here is all you could let yourself know:

You were on a road trip with your best friend.

There was a tent in the backseat and music on the radio.

You were young and free.

What a great time to be young and free in the summer.

What a time to be alive!!

Do not think about what you've done.

Do not think about what you are going to do next.

Do not think about all the steps along the way.

Do not think do not think do not think of anything.

(Do not think about what's in the trunk. And how it got there.)

The trip would take you twenty hours if you drove straight through. Between the money your mom's boyfriend had given you and your earnings from the copy shop, you had 2,746 dollars in cash rolled up in a sock in your duffel bag. A thick stack of bills that felt like play money when you looked at it all together. Like play money for a game. That's all this even was.

The radio was on and your best friend Xavier was humming along to a song he didn't know, staring out the window, and dancing in his seat with his sweatshirt on, and the hood up, because you'd cranked the AC all the way to keep it cold enough, to keep everything in the car very cold. "It's like a meat locker in here!" Xavier had said about the inside of the car. "In a fun way!" *A meat locker.* He was giddy with freedom, with relief, with the fact that you were doing something so sudden and crazy. Giddy with the fact that you were reconnecting after the blip of strangeness that had divided you.

"I can't believe like forty-eight hours ago I was so . . ." He paused. Shook his head. "Actually, it doesn't even matter what I was before. I feel like nothing but right now matters or ever even happened. Do you know what I mean?" He turned to you and smiled. And you told your mouth to smile back, and your mouth agreed and did. On the side of the highway was a sign for a rest stop. "Ooooh, should we stop at McDonald's? Get cones of that stuff that they are legally probably not even allowed to call ice cream because who knows what it even *is*, so they have to just call it *cones*?"

"I'm not hungry yet," you said. You hadn't been hungry in two days and would probably never be hungry again. But more than that, you needed to stay moving, keep moving and never stand still. Standing still was very dangerous.

"Since when does a person have to be hungry to have *cones*?" Xavier said. "C'mon, we can take stylish pics for our Instagrams." He was kidding. He had only ever used Instagram to check Ivy's posts back when he followed her, which he no longer did. And he thought you didn't use it at all.

"Well, you make a good point," you said. Now that you had officially left your body, it was easier to act normal, to agree to things. To do what needed to be done.

You took the next exit, pulled into the lot, parked, walked inside, past the convenience store, past the buckets of salt-water taffy and the penny pressing machine (which under other circumstances you might have wanted to try out, because you loved watching a penny go in as a regular penny and then get pounded and squashed until it was something else entirely). But you had no time for that now. You could not let your thoughts go that deep. You could not consider what you liked and what you did not. It was crowded in that rest stop, everyone on their way to or from somewhere. Just regular people on regular trips. Just like you.

Xavier got into the McDonald's line, and you told him you were going to the bathroom. You went into a stall and took out the phones, the real reason for this stop. The reason you agreed to it. You had to be someone else then, too, you and not you at the same time. You had a text from this guy Steph, who you sort of started dating without quite meaning to. He had written: around this weekend? ☺

Ugh. Im sick in bed! you wrote back.

A second later he wrote:

☹

So sorry to hear!!

I can make you soup!

Well . . . actually, that would probably not help you be less sick. But I can BUY you soup ha ha

Or ice cream?

Or exciting medicines!

Let me know if you need anything or if I can come over

I'm not scared of ur germs . . .

You shut your own phone off then, put it in your pocket. You could not allow yourself to feel anything about this. Anything about anything.

You took out the other phone. The one you kept hidden in the small pocket of your bag, the one you'd deleted one very specific photo off of, the one you tried to forget about while you were driving with Xavier but had to remember now because there was work to do. The sooner anyone knew she was missing, the sooner someone would start trying to find her. And the sooner they might find out that missing was not the only thing she was.

What would happen next? You didn't know.

You can't buy innocence. But you can buy time.

Or, at least, you can try.

There were three new messages in the phone sent to the owner of the phone. You would have to speak for her now, as she could not speak for herself. But first, there was Instagram:

Ivy hadn't posted in a few hours, and she normally posted all the time, every day, all day long. You looked around for something suitable. It was a typical crappy rest stop bathroom—neon-pink soap dribbling from broken soap dispensers, seats sprinkled with pee. There was a machine by the door selling condoms and tampons, glitter temporary tattoos and perfumed towelettes. You took a photo of the machine, which was oddly beautiful when framed just so. The only person who would know these were fake was Xavier. But Xavier didn't follow Ivy. And her account was locked. And he didn't even have a phone.

There was no way he would see this. You hesitated for only a moment before you clicked share. Within seconds, it had thirteen likes and a comment. "Get the tattoos!! Whereya off to?"

But you weren't done. The public part was easy. The private stuff was harder. You looked back at the conversation with Gwen over the last two days. At what you'd already written her so far.

Gwen: 1:15 a.m.: how was your night? You ended up seeing Xavier right?

Gwen: 11:12 a.m.: Uppy uppy you lazy bich

Gwen: 4:45 p.m.: I'm assuming you're just w/ X still and out of batteries . . . but LMK if something terrible has happened to you . . . haha

Gwen: 4:46 p.m.: My dad is being a dick and I'm bored. Let's go to the movies or something????

Gwen: 10:59 p.m.: You know that thing you do where you just stop texting back sometimes? It is laaaaaaaaame

Ivy: 7:20 a.m.: What are you my jealous boyfriend? Calm the fuck down. JK I love you. But I'm a little busy ahem. Never saw Xavier . . . w/ someone else. Can you guess who?

That last text was the first thing Ivy had sent to Gwen since Ivy stopped being Ivy.

You needed to find out what Gwen knew.

Gwen: 10:34 a.m.: I don't know, it could literally be anyone, slut. ☺

Ivy: 11:45 a.m.: Heh, true. But it's only fun if you guess . . .

Where was all this leading? You hadn't figured it out yet. You knew only the next step, and the one after that. You would just have to trust that, when it was time for more steps, your monster brain would figure them out for you. The way it had so far with everything else.

The next message was from Nikolai, the guy whose party you'd gone to. Haven't heard from you in weeks. Are you ignoring me? . . . You deleted that one.

There was one more person to respond to. Ivy's mom.

You took a breath, you steeled yourself.

You were lucky that Ivy had such a history of vanishing, of being bad, of doing whatever she wanted. Her mother didn't even seem worried, just fed up. Since two nights before, her mother had sent a short string of texts, a half dozen or so threatening greater and greater punishments when Ivy finally appeared. But that was it. You looked through the most recent texts:

11:31 p.m.: Come home now or don't come home at all

7:15 a.m.: Calm the fuck down you/Ivy had written back early that morning.

And her mother had written this, moments later: We mean it this time. Now, or do not bother.

Now you wrote: Nope not coming home. Guess that's it.

You swallowed hard as the feelings threatened to bubble up. Ivy had a mother. No matter how angry this mother was, Ivy had a mother who was her mother who would never see her again. And one day, who knew when exactly, her mother would look back at these messages and see what she had said to her daughter and think it was the last thing her daughter ever got from her. It was too terrible, it was too much.

So you found yourself writing one more message back.

Even if you say that, I know you love me. And I love you too.

Your fingers clicked send before you could stop them. You had to be careful, stick to the script. The more you didn't sound like Ivy, the more likely it was that someone would get suspicious, come looking for her—come looking for her before she was ready to be found.

You turned the phone off, put it back in your pocket, and walked out of the bathroom. Xavier was waiting for you right outside, standing there with two cones, holding one out to you, smiling like this was the best day of his whole goddamned life.

Xavier

Xavier spent six hundred miles trying to figure it out.

Six hundred miles of car coffees and bags of Twizzlers and Combos and dangling one arm out the window while the radio blasted. Six hundred miles of sitting there with Sasha next to him gripping the steering wheel, silent and steely like she was alone as they passed through New York and Pennsylvania and Maryland and Virginia. And now, ten hours later, there they were at a campsite in North Carolina, all green grass and tall trees and tents full of parents and kids and dogs with bandannas around their necks. He spent all that time thinking and thinking, and what he was thinking was this: What if all the things he usually felt when he was with Sasha—deep connection, unconditional understanding, total comfort, delight at just *being* with her—weren't just friend feelings? What if they were something else? And they had been all along?

They parked and got out of the car. Sasha took the tent from the backseat and brought it over to the campsite without letting him help. He watched her. Her jaw was set, gaze distant.

Xavier had made so many mistakes. He realized that now.

The night of his birthday, when Ivy had found him, he shouldn't have gone outside with her. He shouldn't have messed with her at all. He should have stayed with Sasha, taken her somewhere and looked her straight in the eye, and said, "It's scary to let things get weird, but maybe we should try it." It would have changed things. It would have changed everything.

What if it was too late?

The sun was down and someone at the next campsite over was playing a guitar. Xavier walked back from the woods toward their tent. Through the thin netting of the door, he could see a glow of a screen, her phone. *But one rule,* she'd said. *No phones.* So what was she doing with hers?

She looked up when Xavier entered. They'd barely spoken in hours. Xavier wasn't sure how to act now, not after everything he'd been thinking. She slipped the phone under her thigh so Xavier wouldn't see. He felt the sticky fingers of jealousy uncurling in his belly. But what right did he have to be jealous, after everything? Still, he couldn't help but wonder who she was talking to. Steph? Had she been texting with him this whole time?

Suddenly, Xavier knew he had to get out of that tent. Sasha

had said they didn't need to make a fire. They had peanut but-
ter and bread from a rest stop convenience store, apples, and a
jug of water. There was nothing to cook. But there was a fire
pit right there, so Xavier gathered up sticks while he tried to
slow his racing heart. He found old newspaper in the trash and
started twisting the pages into kindling. He wanted to be use-
ful and needed something to do with his hands. Sasha came
out of the tent.

"Did I ever tell you how I was a Boy Scout?" Xavier said. "I
must have, right? Top-notch fire starter."

"I don't know," she said. She stared at him like he was a
stranger.

"Hi, my name's Xavier. Nice to meet you." Xavier held out
his hand for her to shake and she shook it, and when their
hands touched, he had the almost overwhelming urge to lean
forward and kiss her. She quickly pulled her hand away and
stepped back, like she was reading his mind maybe. Or like she
was thinking about something else entirely.

It was late and the fire was out. They were inside the tent. Sasha
had unzipped her sleeping bag and spread it across the floor.
Xavier had his sweatshirt balled up behind his head for a pillow.
He was lying on his back. They were in the dark, close together,
breathing in the same warm tent-scented air. They had slept
this close a couple times before—it had never meant anything.
But somehow, now, it felt different. Maybe it was time to say

something. Maybe now was the time to tell her what he'd been thinking.

"Hey," he said. "Have you . . ."—*ever thought about what would happen if we*—". . . fallen asleep yet?"

There was rustling. "Not yet," she said. Xavier turned on the little camping lantern and the close space was filled with dim light. Sasha rolled over. She looked like maybe she'd been crying. Or maybe she'd been trying very hard not to.

"Whatever it is, whatever is bothering you," he said. "I know I promised I wouldn't ask about it, but I want you to know I'm here. To help, to figure out, whatever it is. I'm here, same as all those times you were there for me."

Sasha nodded ever so slightly. She seemed scared.

"You can tell me anything, you know that, right?" Xavier stared at her until she nodded again. But she wasn't looking at him anymore.

"I'm fine," she said. He could tell she was lying. "I just want to go to sleep."

They lay there in the dark, not talking, not touching. And Xavier knew it was not the time to bring anything up. Now was the time to lie in silence with his outstretched hand open between them. If she reached hers out in the night, his would be there.

Sasha

At some point, the dark wall of the tent started to lighten. The sun was coming up and it was time to go. You were not sure if you'd slept at all as you lay on the ground next to Xavier. If you are tired enough, being conscious and being unconscious feel the same. You waited as the hours passed, your head filled with awful images you did not want to see. You were either thinking or dreaming, and it was impossible to tell which.

Xavier snored quietly a few feet away. You went outside, you peed behind a tree. You came back and opened the jug of water and gulped and gulped. Water in and water out. You imagined it purifying you, washing you clean. But of course no amount of water could do that.

Just over seven hundred miles to go. You had been going fast, but you needed to go faster. There were things to outrun. The smell, for example. And your conscience, which might catch up with you sooner than you'd hoped. For now, you would shut your brain off, shut your heart off. If you drove straight through, you could be there by nightfall. You could not let yourself think of anything but that. Seven hundred more miles of gritted teeth and thoughts banished from your brain.

That's all you had to get through.

Well, that and the rest of your life.

You were still trying your best to pretend. You were trying, trying, trying, but it was getting harder. Your brain didn't want to comply anymore, your body didn't either. Your chest felt tight, your head wrapped in cotton, and you could not think. The truth was jagged rocks under your skin, barely below the surface, and they kept coming up, up, up, threatening to break through.

You looked at Xavier in the dim light while he slept. You knew that you had loved that face very much very recently, that you had loved it more than any you'd ever seen in your life. But right there, in that tent, you could not access those feelings at all. You could not access any feelings, really. Looking at him by the light of the early morning sun through the walls of the tent, he did not look like your best friend or someone you loved. He did not look like anything.

"Hey," you said. "Xavier."

He rolled over. Blinking, he started to smile.

"It's time to go."

He yawned and stretched.

"Maybe we can stop at a drive-through," he said. "Delicious fast-food breakfast is the greatest."

You had not really eaten in days. You had not slept in days. You made yourself drink water because water was necessary. You made yourself breathe because air was necessary. You breathed in and out. Air was very necessary.

Without air, you would die.

Back in the car. There was a smell now. Maybe because it had been so warm the night before. Sweet rot.

Xavier sniffed, but was silent.

You gagged, but there was nothing in your stomach to throw up. So it was decided: you would try not to breathe. Maybe you could do without air, too.

Xavier

They sat together in that swiftly moving metal box. Still, Sasha barely spoke. Xavier's heart hammered, as though he was running all those miles they crossed, running and running, legs pumping, chasing after Sasha, who kept getting farther away.

He had not changed his clothes or brushed his teeth or showered. He was self-conscious, sitting in the car for so many hours, so dirty and so close to Sasha. He'd never been self-conscious around Sasha before. Did he smell? Something in the car smelled, that was for sure.

They stopped for gas at a rest stop. Xavier bought a travel-size toothpaste and a toothbrush and deodorant and a fresh T-shirt. He washed his face in the bathroom with hand soap and brushed his teeth, put on deodorant and threw his old shirt in the trash. He bought an apple-cinnamon air-freshener tree for the rearview mirror to give Sasha as a joke.

He got back in the car. "Got you a present," he said. "So you don't have to smell me." He handed it to her. She didn't even crack a smile.

They drove. They stopped at more rest stops, and Sasha continued the secret phone stuff she thought Xavier didn't know about. She was texting Steph, Xavier was sure of that now. Xavier wanted to ask her about it, but knew he couldn't. What could have happened between her and Steph in such a short amount of time? What could have happened that had made her have to run away? Had he hurt her? Xavier felt his hands curling into fists at the idea of it.

If Steph had hurt Sasha, Xavier would kill him.

They drove and drove and drove. Three hundred, four hundred, five hundred, six hundred, an impossible amount of miles zipped by under them. Sasha's eyes were ringed in red. He offered to take over driving for a while. "You must be so tired," he said. "Do you want to at least rest a little?" But she just shook her head.

They passed through North Carolina, South Carolina, and Georgia. They crossed into Florida and Sasha kept going. Xavier began to wonder if she even had a destination in mind. Maybe her plan was to keep driving until they went straight into the ocean. But when they reached the exit for the Florida Everglades, Sasha got off the highway and followed the signs until they were there. She eased the car through lush overhanging trees, past big blue lakes topped with a frosting of green algae. She exhaled. Maybe this was what they'd been heading toward all along. It certainly was beautiful.

Sasha got out to pay the entrance fee.

The sun was low in the sky, and the air in the car smelled like apples and cinnamon over top of that odd scent he could not place. Xavier sniffed himself and determined that he wasn't the source of the stink. He remembered the time, many years ago, when a mouse had died in one of his family's kitchen cabinets. It smelled worse and worse until they figured out what it was and his mom took the dead mouse outside to dispose of it. *How strange,* Xavier thought. *How strange that this kind of smells like that.*

Sasha

Leave your body and don't crack. Do what you need to do, watch from outside, don't feel, don't think. You are not here. You are far away, operating the puppet hands that are your hands, operating the puppet legs that are your legs, the puppet mouth, the puppet heart. Do what you need to do.

Leave your body and feel nothing.

Leave your body just like she did.

Xavier

They were inside the tent, camped again for the night, and Xavier was reading out loud. "... in the vast expanse of blackness, there was a great and mighty roar. Space Captain Jones looked out the window of the ship and ..." He had found a paperback book abandoned on a picnic bench, an old pulp sci-fi novel with planets and dinosaurs on the cover. He had hoped maybe they could revel together in its silliness, that it could be a fun, meaningless thing to distract Sasha from whatever was going on. But Sasha did not seem to be listening, and when she thought he wasn't looking, she kept checking her phone, which he wasn't even supposed to know she had with her. He went on reading, but after a while Sasha closed her eyes. "Sasha?" She didn't answer, so he switched off the lantern. He heard her moving around then, like she was probably awake after all. He lay there for a while, wondering why she would pretend to be sleeping, until finally he drifted off himself.

He dreamed they were in the car, but the car was full of soil, and flowers were growing thick out of the deep, damp earth in the back. Xavier and Sasha sat up in the front as the vines writhed and twisted behind them. He knew the vines were there, but he couldn't see them, couldn't see them until they slithered up front and wrapped themselves around their throats.

Sasha

At first, you could not even bring yourself to touch her.

You had snuck out of the tent while Xavier slept, gotten back in the car, drove in the silvery gray of dawn breaking. You got out and stood in front of the trunk. Then there you were, with the birds, crickets, animals rustling, loud life all around you, but you were alone. A hot wind blew and you took a breath to steady yourself, shallow through your mouth so you wouldn't have to smell her.

There was no turning back now. You had done your research, picked the perfect place, made your way there. You kept her alive through her phone so that no one would start looking yet.

There was one final step. You had to do this now. Everything had been leading to this.

You reached out, felt the scratchy wool, the solid mass beneath it. You pulled back, your stomach turned over. You leaned down with your hands on your knees, gagged up bile, swallowed it down. Took a long deep breath. Told yourself to fucking pull it together, but you weren't sure you could. Not this time.

The first time you touched her, back there in the woods, it hadn't been real. You were far away from yourself and you could not feel anything, not the weight of her, or what it meant. You watched yourself from a thousand miles away as you lifted her up, up, up, like she barely weighed anything at all. You had always felt so strong, hard muscles, big arms, thick thighs. You had always been proud of that.

Things were different now. Standing there in the warm, damp air as the sun rose over the horizon, you were made of glass, about to break. You were about to shatter into so many pieces that you could never be put back together. But that couldn't happen yet.

You thought of Xavier back in that tent, you thought of him quiet and still in the dark, so worried about you, with no clue of what had happened. You thought of the uncertain future ahead of him, ahead of both of you. You thought of how hard you would try to forget what you were about to do, but you had a flash of understanding then: you would remember every detail of this forever. Neither time nor wishing nor desperation would fade it.

You would always remember leaning into the trunk, taking a breath, wrapping your arms around her, and lifting the sturdy weight of her, unwieldy beneath the blanket. The stench of her rising up over the musty wool.

You would remember how your every muscle strained as you staggered toward the lake, how your sneakers sank farther into damp earth the closer you got. Your arms started to shake, but you kept going. You tried to leave your body. You did not want to have to feel this, but you were locked inside that moment. And there was no way out.

You would always remember how you put her down a few feet out into the lake, how you tried to be gentle, as though she could still feel it. The blanket shifted, and there was her face in the blue dawn light. Eyes blankly open, skin mottled, lips parted. You felt the sobs tightening your chest, rising up to choke you. You gathered rocks from along the shoreline, filled up the pockets of her cutoffs, the pockets of her sweatshirt, packing them full, praying they would be enough. She was so heavy then, and you lifted her legs, gagging as you touched her skin. You put her feet beneath your arms and dragged her in. You would remember how you had to close your eyes, because you could not bear to look at her, could not have continued if you had.

You would always remember the water rising up to your shins, your knees, higher, higher, the same temperature as the air around you. You turned back, and Ivy was fully submerged, the lake and the light playing tricks with her face.

You thought of people drowning. You thought of babies

swimming in their mothers' bellies. You thought of Ivy at that party, out on the grass in the dark, twisting and swaying, so beautiful when she danced, like she was underwater.

You would always remember when you were in chest-deep, how you opened your eyes, dunked down, wrapped your arms around her, held her tight. You kicked as hard as you could, fighting against the weight of the rocks, the lake ready to claim her. The tears were streaming down your cheeks then. The sky was orange and pink and gold, the surface of the water a shifting, swirling mirror.

You would always remember how you held her tightly.

How you whispered, *I'm sorry.*

And then you let her go.

Xavier

Xavier woke to the soft *zzzzt* of the tent being unzipped. He looked up just in time to see Sasha reaching one arm in for her duffel, the cool light of dawn behind her. Her clothes were soaking. She was covered in mud. He sat up. His heart was pounding.

"Whoa, what happened," Xavier said. "Are you okay?"

She didn't answer.

"Did you fall in a lake?"

She shook her head.

"Did you go swimming?" he asked.

She stared at him blankly and shook her head again. "I need to take a shower."

She walked away from the tent toward the shower cabin, toward the slowly rising sun. He was so confused and worried that he crept out of the tent to follow her. He stood outside the bathroom and leaned against the wooden wall. He sat down on the ground and waited for her. She emerged a long time later, clean, hair wet, wearing fresh shorts and a T-shirt. Her skin was pink, like maybe she'd been trying to scrub it right off.

She saw him. Blinked for a moment, as if she barely even knew who he was. "I was worried," Xavier said.

"Thank you," she said.

"Where are your wet clothes?" he said.

"I threw them away."

He wanted to beg her for answers, for some explanation. But he knew he couldn't.

They went back to the tent. The sun was fully up now, the birds screaming loudly. There was a dog barking off in the distance. Xavier wanted to tell her everything he'd realized, everything he'd been thinking—the mistakes they'd made with each other and about each other, and how maybe it was not too late to fix them.

She started breaking down the tent. "Let's go home," she said. And he felt then a flood of relief, because some part of him had thought that maybe she was not ever planning on going back. Something was still wrong, still very wrong, but if she was going home, it would be okay. He would make it okay. He had to.

I knew something was wrong as soon as I got those texts. Those first texts from Ivy that did not even sound like her. I knew something was TERRIBLY WRONG and NOT RIGHT AT ALL. I breathed deep, like that dumb shrink told me once, to calm down. BREATHED IN AND OUT, THE TWO BEST DIRECTIONS TO BREATHE. But nothing helped.

WHAT IS GOING ON HERE?

HOW DO I STOP THIS?

I wrote to this not-quite-Ivy: where ARE you even?

No answer. So I had to figure out the answer ON MY OWN. I was ALL ON MY OWN AGAIN.

Her Instagram had been updated with pictures she would never post. One was from a rest stop south on I-95 with a million comments under it from DUMB DUMMIES who thought it was really hers.

As soon as I saw that very first picture, I got in my car and I started to drive.

Drive drive drive

DRIVE DRIVE DRIVE

I sent texts along the way and sometimes she texted back.

AND SOMETIMES SHE DID NOT.

But it didn't even matter once I figured out the pattern. Which was less a pattern and more just a line going STRAIGHT DOWN TO THE BOTTOM.

So I followed it.

Xavier

Four hours later, Sasha was trying so hard to pretend to be holding it together, but she was on the verge of losing it entirely. Xavier had melted down himself—he recognized the signs. And besides, she was his very best friend, possibly much more than that, as it turned out. He knew her better than she thought.

They'd driven for two full days, plus four hours more, almost fifteen hundred miles. They'd eaten only rest-stop food and spent two nights lying on the hard ground while Sasha did a pretty unconvincing job of pretending to be asleep. Even if she wouldn't tell him what was wrong, wouldn't even give him the tiniest hint of a clue, Xavier knew two things for sure—Sasha needed real food and she needed real sleep.

"Please," he said. "Can we stop? Anywhere with beds, the next motel we pass. Just for a few hours, so you can rest. I don't have money with me, but I'll pay you back as soon as we get home, I swear I will."

And she looked like she was about to say no, but then instead she nodded, and they pulled off the highway and stopped at the first place they found. It was perfect. THE MERMAID HIDEAWAY MOTEL was printed on the big plate-glass front window in swirly script letters that were probably supposed to look like waves from the sea. And Xavier thought about how it would definitely be a great place for a mermaid to hide, because it was actually pretty far from the ocean really. Xavier turned to Sasha to make a joke about this, but then changed his mind.

The parking lot was entirely empty.

The lobby was empty, too, small and hot with an ancient air conditioner coughing in the corner and a worn turquoise carpet on the floor. There was a big glass table on the side near the huge window and a glass vase filled with fake flowers sitting in the middle. Sasha was staring at it, unblinking, like a mannequin. She pulled her phone out of her pocket and took a picture of the vase and the flowers. She didn't seem to remember that she was trying to hide it from Xavier.

Finally, a guy appeared at the desk, only a few years older than they were. Xavier talked to him while Sasha kept staring at those fake flowers. He said a room would be $110 for the night. Usually check-in wasn't until three, but considering the hotel was entirely vacant, they could check in now if they wanted, and he would need a credit card for a deposit. Sasha said, well, we don't have one of those, but what if we paid forty dollars extra in cash? The guy looked around to make sure no one else was watching, and he said okay. Xavier didn't think the guy even officially checked them in, he just put the cash in his pocket and gave them the room key, not a key card because of how old the place was.

"Breakfast is seven to ten," he said. "The pool is open till midnight, but use at your own risk. There's no lifeguard, and honestly, I'm not sure the last time that thing was cleaned."

Xavier promised he would pay Sasha back as soon as they got home, but she said not to worry about it. When the front desk kid couldn't see, she peeled bills off a huge roll of cash.

"Whoa, Nelly . . . ," Xavier said.

"From my job and Marc," she said. And Xavier wondered if when she'd originally left she had planned on being gone for much longer. Maybe if he hadn't gone with her, she'd never have come back at all.

They climbed a narrow set of stairs. The higher they went, the hotter it got. It was just before noon, but Xavier felt outside of time, and just barely on earth.

Their room was at the end of a hallway. He slipped the key into the lock and turned. The room was small and dim, cheesy and chintzy, but Xavier loved everything about it—the seashell lamp, the aqua walls, the framed blotchy seaside scene. There was only one bed, covered in a thin white duvet and a mountain of pillows. Being alone with Sasha in that room somehow felt more alone than alone in the car, alone in the tent. Sasha sat down on the bed and stared at the wall. He thought of the time when their positions had been switched, him barely functional, Sasha taking care of him.

"Sasha?" Xavier said. He went over to her, stood next to her, unsure what to do with his hands. *Where did you go?* She turned, looked at him, but did not seem to see him. *Please come back.*

"I'm so tired," she said. And she slipped off her shoes and got under the covers. A few minutes later, she was fast asleep.

I drove and drove, following the eensy little bread crumbs from PLACE to PLACE to PLACE, and when the crumbs stopped, I JUST KEPT DRIVING.

Sometimes we texted, me and Ivy/me and "IVY."

I checked Instagram, looked at more posts she never would have posted. Responded to more texts she NEVER WOULD HAVE WRITTEN. Kept pretending and pretending to think "IVY" was Ivy. I am so good at pretending.

WHAT WILL I FIND WHEN I FINALLY CATCH UP?

I know what I want to BELIEVE, but it is DANGEROUS to WANT to believe a thing, because then your DUMB STUPID

IDIOT BRAIN finds things to make the thing you want to be true look true EVEN IF IT ISN'T. If you were a LITTLE FISHY living in the BIG OCEAN and your GREATEST WISH was to be EATEN BY A SHARK, well even a tired octopus would start to look VERY SHARKY to you. EVENTUALLY you'd see those TENTACLE SUCKERS, and they'd look like TEETH, they'd look like SHARP SHARK TEETH. If you know what I'm saying.

So I DROVE and DROVE and told my brain SHUT RIGHT UP, YOU ARE NOT WELCOME HERE.

HOPE WILL KILL YOU, that much I know.

But other things will kill you faster.

Xavier

Sasha slept and slept, flat on her back, lips slightly parted. She looked like a character from a fairy tale, someone under a spell. Pale sunlight filtered through the windows right onto her face, but she did not stir. Xavier watched her, then decided it was creepy to watch someone sleep, so he forced himself to turn away. When he turned back, the sun had gone behind a cloud and the light in the room was dim. For a moment, his heart pounded. She was so still, she looked dead.

Xavier shook his head.

He had to get out of that room, he decided. He was going a little crazy. Xavier went downstairs. There was no one there. He heard the *bing*ing and *ping*ing of a handheld video game coming from a room off the side of the front desk, but that was it. He sat in a chair in the lobby and read an old water-wrinkled magazine about sailboats and a catalog for aboveground swimming pools. He stared at the huge plate-glass window facing the street, at the backs of the gold and blue letters, at the fake palm tree, at the fake flower arrangements. Across the empty parking lot and across the freeway were a convenience store and a gas station. Xavier walked outside. He was hungry. He bought a tiny little pizza that was spinning slowly in a heated case next to two very shiny hot dogs. He bought a large orange soda. He searched for a present for Sasha, something fun for when she woke up. There were bags of shark-shaped gummies and he got one. He imagined opening up the bag and lining the gummies up on the window. Xavier imagined her smiling when she saw them. *Sasha, watch out! Shark attack!!* is what he'd say.

She was still asleep when Xavier got back.

He went downstairs and ate in the lobby, sitting on a very scratchy chair. The guy at the front desk was back now, talking on the phone to someone with very bad reception, he was saying, "Not bloated—LOA-DED. I said it is LOA-DED." Xavier sort of wished he had his own phone with him.

More hours passed. He sat and he waited and he wondered if he would tell Sasha the truth when she woke up. He closed his eyes and tried to imagine doing so, but it seemed impossible.

Xavier climbed those hot stairs again. It was late afternoon now. He tried to be as quiet as he could, but when he opened the door, Sasha opened her eyes.

She sat up, moving in slow motion like she was underwater. "What time is it?" she said. Her voice was thick with sleep. She rubbed her eyes.

"Four fifteen," Xavier said. "You snoozed for a really long time. You seemed like you needed it."

She swallowed, then looked blankly around the room.

"There's a convenience store across the street, pretty decent food if you like E. coli on your pizza. . . ."

Xavier stopped and stared at her. Even like that, hair in her face, eyes puffy, lips dry, she was the most beautiful thing he'd ever seen. He took a breath. It wasn't the right time to tell her, he knew that. But what if there was no such thing as the right time? What if the part of him that told him there was, was the same as the part of him that kept him from figuring out how he felt in the first place, that kept him from kissing her those times he wanted to/could have/should have?

Telling her would change things. But maybe that was okay.

Ignore your sweaty hands, ignore your dry mouth, the pounding of your desperate heart.

"Sasha, listen. I know this is going to sound like it's coming out of nowhere. Or maybe it won't. Or maybe it will sound crazy. . . ." The words fell out of his mouth without waiting for him to even think them. "Maybe you already know what I'm about to say, but . . . We've been friends for a while and during that time I was so preoccupied with . . ." But no, he didn't want to mention Ivy at all, not now. He felt his face growing hot.

He forced himself to look up at her. He had to be brave. She deserved for him to be brave. "I feel like maybe . . ." *Say it. Say it. JUST SAY IT.*

"Xavier."

Sasha was staring back at him, eyes wide, entirely unreadable. Was that excitement? Hope? Happiness? Horror? Did she know what he was about to say? She must know. She knew. Xavier couldn't breathe.

"Xavier," she said again. She stood up from the bed, walked toward him, looking at him like she'd never seen him before in her life. Did she want him to say it or was she trying to stop him?

She had the strangest expression on her face, and Xavier had no idea what it meant.

"Can I . . . kiss you?" He heard the words as he said them.

She just stayed there blinking, like she could not understand what he was saying. She opened her mouth and then snapped it shut.

"I'm sorry," Xavier said. "I don't mean to make things weird. . . ."

She stared at him and slowly nodded.

"You're sure?" Xavier said.

She nodded again.

And he knew then that she was just scared, too, scared the way he had been for so long.

"There is nothing to be afraid of," Xavier told her. "I promise."

Their lips were five feet apart, four feet, three feet, two feet, one foot, one inch. Xavier paused.

This is actually happening, Xavier told himself. *Don't ever forget this moment.*

And then he kissed her.

There they were, lips against lips, his body was on fire.

"Is this okay?" Xavier said.

She pulled back a few inches, just enough to look him in the eye. And she seemed for a second unsure, but she said, "Yes. I've wanted this for so long." And then they were kissing again, fast and hard, desperate and urgent, like this was their one chance, like they were running out of time.

I was sitting in the car in the parking lot of a GODDAMN MCDONALD'S, and I was holding my lucky penny that I got at a PENNY-SQUISHING MACHINE at a REST STOP and STARING at it, and what I was thinking was MAYBE IT IS BROKEN, because it is TOO GODDAMN HOT here in this car far from home in this HOT PLACE where I had never even been before and did not think I would like to go again.

Maybe my penny stopped working or maybe the luck has drained RIGHT OUT OF IT, because of the HEAT and the SWEAT, and oh, I am only kidding. I DID NOT BELIEVE IN MY LUCKY PENNY, ANYWAY.

"IVY" had not posted in MANY, MANY HOURS, and "IVY" had not written me back EITHER. And it occurred to me then, WHAT

IF THIS IVY JUST DISAPPEARS. What if "IVY" STOPS WRITING BACK ENTIRELY, the way she always USED TO DO, which I hated the VERY MOST? The problem was, in the past when Ivy vanished, I knew she'd always come back. And this time, well, THIS TIME I COULD NOT SAY THAT. I looked at my phone, LOOKED and LOOKED and LOOKED, and then went to Instagram and pulled that little wall of photos down and released it JUST IN CASE there was a new one since the last time I checked one-and-one-half minutes before. BUT THERE WERE NO NEW ONES. PULL and RELEASE and PULL and RELEASE. But NOTHNG WAS HAPPENING AND I WAS NOT FEELING VERY GOOD. I was feeling VERY BAD ACTUALLY, if you want to know the truth.

I told myself to CALM DOWN. I told myself to TAKE A BREATH. I even said these things OUT LOUD to myself in the CAR in the MCDONALD'S PARKING LOT, which should give you some idea of how bad it had gotten.

I WAITED AND WAITED AND WAITED. My stomach was twisting around like it was full of WORMS and SNAKES. I looked at that AWFUL LAST PICTURE that helped me NOT AT ALL. A shiny table, blue plastic flowers, a chipped white vase. The flowers were worse than dead. THEY WERE NEVER EVEN ALIVE. I stared at the picture and stared at it. It wasn't even CAPTIONED. It was just THERE. There was no GEO-TAG,

*and Ivy had stopped answering my TEXTS. WHAT THE
ACTUAL FUCK? THIS WOULD NOT HELP ME AT ALL.*

*So I forced myself to look at the pictures that were already there to
pass the time: the gummy peaches in Georgia, the coffee in South
Carolina, the rest stops, and the ice-cream cones. Some of these
things, they could have been from her. They really could have been.
Ivy LOVED gummies. I LOVE TO CHEW, she said once. MY
ANIMAL BRAIN thinks if I'm CHEWING this much, I must
be eating an ANIMAL I HUNTED and KILLED, and it is
rewarding me for it. But Ivy thought meat was mean . . . one of the
few, maybe the VERY ONLY things that Ivy did to be nice was not
eat meat. GUMMIES HAVE GELATIN, I told her once when
I was mad at her for a reason I cannot even remember, but I am
sure it was very valid. THEY ARE NOT VEGETARIAN. She
shrugged. I'M NOT A VEGETARIAN, I JUST DON'T EAT
ANYTHING THAT MAKES ME FEEL GUILTY. AND I
FEEL FINE EATING THESE. I FEEL GREAT. It was perfect
Ivy logic. So messed up that you almost had to respect it. ALMOST.*

Xavier

Her hands were moving up under the back of his shirt, their clothes were coming off piece by piece in that warm, dim room. Then Xavier's shirt was on the floor and hers was, too, and they were pressed together, and her skin was so warm, and they tumbled onto the bed. Xavier was on top, he pushed himself up on one arm to look at her. Her eyes were closed. His heart squeezed in his chest. It seemed to him that perhaps his entire life had been building toward this moment, of him in bed with Sasha, his favorite person, who as it turned out was exactly what he'd always been looking for. He felt his lips curve into a smile. Her eyes were still closed.

"This is so . . . ," he said. But he couldn't even finish.

This was what?

This was everything.

He didn't want to rush it. He wanted to remember every second.

He ran his fingers over her lower lip and across her jaw, traced the curve of her collarbone with his thumb.

He looked at that locket around her neck, at the bronze chain against her smooth skin, and felt a wave of tenderness. It was the one her grandmother had given her, the one she always wore. He thought about how tender and tough Sasha was. How much she cared about the people she loved. He reached out to stroke it, ran his fingers gently across her throat, wrapped his fingers softly around her neck, and leaned down to kiss her.

Sasha's eyes popped open. She sat up, her face frozen in a mask of pure horror.

"Oh my god," she whispered. "What the fuck am I doing?"

Xavier's stomach twisted. What was happening?

"I can't. Not after everything."

She got out of bed and started gathering up her clothes. She pulled her tank top over her head, pulled her shorts up her legs, shoved her feet into her shoes.

"Sasha, please. You have to tell me what's happening. Don't run away again! Is it because of Steph? Is this because of . . ."

But he didn't even get to finish his question. She was already out the door.

Sasha

Out in the hot, empty parking lot, hands on knees, gut punched, bent over heaving, ragged raw. That was how it happened, that was how I got back into my body, gasping for air, finding nothing. Those blue hairs, Xavier's hairs—I could feel them now, sliding from my stomach, uncurling, skinny blue snakes crawling up.

I gagged.

I raised my hand to my throat.

Choked.

There was the truth. I could not hide from it. I could not run from it. I could not imagine it away.

I thought of Xavier back there in the hotel room, his skin smooth and warm, body pressed against mine. At first, I'd felt nothing at all. . . .

His fingers around my throat, that's what finally broke me.

Just like what broke Ivy.

What did he do?

What have I done?

I'd been running on pure adrenaline, pure terror, no sleep, outside of my body. And then the thing I'd desperately wanted for so long started happening. But it wasn't what I wanted at all. Not anymore. The shell I'd built around myself broke open and everything came out:

Xavier killed Ivy.

And I covered it up.

I gagged again, spit up sour bile. And then I started to run. My feet pounded the ground as the sun went down. I could feel the heat of the day coming up from the road. Headlights flipped on. Horns honked. Thoughts exploded in my brain like firecrackers.

All along I'd been trying so hard to protect him, to protect him from the consequences of what he'd done, protect him even from the knowledge of it. But why?

Fuck fuck fuck fuck fuck.

What made what he did somehow okay? Because he was my friend? Because he was a *"nice guy"*? Because he was messed up when he did it? Because I was in love with him?

I thought of times I'd heard of someone offering excuses where there were none. The girl in the article defending her rapist friend because his victim was drunk, the mother of the boy at school who hit his girlfriend saying relationships are complicated, the murderer's father on the news claiming his son was just a naive kid who made a mistake.

And in that moment, I understood something:

The faraway monster always looks different than the monster in front of you, in your arms, in your heart. When someone you cherish does something incomprehensible, you will find reasons to decide they are the exception. You will cling to the details, tell yourself, *but this is different*. But it never is.

No one thinks the people they love are monsters. Because love is the biggest liar of all.

I closed my eyes and felt the weight of her in my arms, felt the damp fabric of her sweatshirt as I packed it full of rocks.

Holy fuck. I was losing my mind.

Maybe I'd already lost it. Maybe I'd lost it when I took Xavier's hairs and swallowed them down, or before that, in the woods along with my necklace. Maybe I'd lost it at Sloe Joe's the moment Ivy came in, tiny and wiry and so alive on the day I was about to tell Xavier the truth.

Xavier killed Ivy.

And I put her body in a lake.

And there was no taking it back.

You can just never take anything back.

The pavement under me shifted. My hands slammed into the blacktop, tiny rocks jammed into my palms. I stayed like that, hands and knees pressed to the road.

I closed my eyes tight. The whole time I was worried about

what would happen when he finally found out Ivy was dead. Or if he ever understood what he'd done.

What I wasn't counting on was this: how I'd feel when I faced it myself.

What the fuck was I going to do now?

When I was a kid I used to try and melt ice with my EYES. I would take a cube out and put it on the table. I would STARE and STARE and STARE and pretend that my eyes were shooting LASERS that would turn the ICE into WATER. And do you know what?

IT WORKED.

Now maybe you will say, BUT IT WOULD HAVE TURNED TO WATER, ANYWAY. THAT IS what ice DOES, it MELTS. Well, I will say, WHAT ARE YOU an ICE PROFESSOR? You can CHANGE things just by LOOKING at them is my point. And THAT is what happened that day in the car with that dumb picture that looked like nothing at all, LESS than nothing. WORSE than nothing. Because then suddenly it was everything.

THERE in the BLUE SCRIPT. RIGHT THERE in the reflection of that shiny table with the sad chipped vase and the worse-than-dead flowers. There were now letters that I SWEAR WERE NOT THERE BEFORE. The letters on the TABLE said LETOM YAWAEDIH DIAMREM EHT. And I thought, well HMM, WHAT LANGUAGE IS THAT IN. I thought, IS THIS IN ANOTHER COUNTRY and WHERE ARE THEY. And I stared and stared at those letters, and then I realized they were a REFLECTION, so they were BACKWARD. And then I looked at them, and I made them forward with my eyes, and I did an Internet search, and the ANSWER was right there WAITING FOR ME.

And I started to drive.

Xavier

Xavier knew he had no right to be jealous. It was his own fault for being so slow, so hesitant, so unsure for so long. But when had jealousy ever listened to reason?

"Not after everything . . . ," she'd said. The truth uncurled in his belly, climbing up his throat, and Xavier was choking on it: she meant, *not after Steph.* Xavier suddenly realized that the past few days, every strange moment that Xavier didn't understand—her leaving home in the first place, lying awake in that tent all night, running out now—it was about Steph. All of it was because of him, Steph was who she cared about now, who was at the center of her mind and heart. If Xavier ever had a chance with her, it was gone. He was too late.

He sat on the bed they had been in together only moments before. Nothing seemed real. Xavier pictured Steph's blandly handsome face, his broad shoulders, and solid arms. He pictured those arms wrapping around Sasha, squeezing her tight.

Xavier was still half naked. He gathered up his clothes, put them on slowly. Should he follow her? Should he wait for her to come back? *Would* she come back?

Xavier could not sit in this room without her. He bent down to slip on his shoes, and that's when Xavier saw the phone. Sasha's phone on the floor, which must have slipped out when their clothes were coming off.

Everything he'd been wondering about this whole trip, the answers were in there. Xavier knew he shouldn't look—he knew that—but he couldn't help it.

Xavier picked it up.

He glanced at the last text Sasha had gotten. But it wasn't from Steph. It was from . . . Gwen? Xavier turned away without reading it. He knew they'd been friends once a long time ago, but it certainly seemed strange that Sasha would be texting with her now—and not even mention it to him. Not that Sasha owed him an explanation, of course, she didn't, but . . .

Xavier looked back at her phone.

Ivy, is something up?

Ivy? Xavier stared at the phone, with the message from Gwen on the screen, a little crack in the corner.

The little crack in the corner from when someone had dropped it at a party.

This wasn't Sasha's phone at all.

They say in a sensory-deprivation chamber, eventually a person starts hallucinating. Their HEAD fills their BRAIN with pictures that are not there. The thoughts COME and KEEP COMING and no one can STOP THEM. WELL the SAME goes for driving. After a certain amount of driving alone, a person starts to go a little crazy maybe.

I told myself stories to fill up the time, to keep the thoughts I did not want to come from coming. I told myself stories to drown out the other ones.

There once was a girl named Ivy who went into the woods to cheat on her boyfriend. She went to cheat with a guy named Jake. He was handsome and funny and strange in just the right ways. Strange in just the ways she liked. She met him there in those woods, but he did not stay long. He did not stay long out there with her in those woods.

Ivy had had plans with her boyfriend, Xavier, that night, but she decided they didn't matter when she made her plans with Jake. Or maybe they DID matter and her broken plans were kind of the point. Maybe she wanted to get caught, was hoping to all along. Maybe she liked Xavier best when she could sense the needy, hungry panic, liked him best when he was jealous and would do anything on earth to keep her. She liked him best when he was a wild animal, and she had made him that way.

So she went to the woods. She saw Xavier's many messages and ignored them. They kept coming, those messages, buzz buzz buzzing . . . she watched them and waited to see, each one more panicked then the last. And the crazier he went, the more she smiled. The more she felt finally complete.

She was alone by then. She waited in the woods alone, smoking a joint, sitting in that tire swing and spinning around. She planned to text Xavier eventually, but she lost track of time, the woods were so nice right then.

She stayed and she waited. And then just like that, Xavier appeared.

He was drunk and crazier maybe than she'd ever seen him. He was furious and wild.

His eyes did not look right.

She decided she was glad he was there. She thought that maybe he'd finally fuck her in that angry way she liked, in that angry way she had gotten others to do. But never him, never sweet, gentle Xavier, who genuinely did not seem to want to grab her by the throat and slam her against a wall like some other guys did. She thought maybe this time finally he would.

They started kissing. She got him to put his hands around her throat. She got him to put his hands there, and squeeze and squeeze.

But then he would not stop.

She grabbed his hair, tried to push him off her. She couldn't breathe. And she needed to breathe. What she needed more than anything she'd ever needed before in her life was to breathe. But he did not let go.

And so she did not get to.

Xavier

Xavier went outside and stood in the parking lot. He waited and waited for Sasha. And then there she was, walking up from the road, face flushed. Their eyes locked and neither of them smiled.

Forty minutes ago they had been up in that hotel room, clothes everywhere, hands everywhere, and he'd almost told her he loved her. But the two people in that room did not exist anymore.

Xavier held out the phone.

"How did you get that?" she said.

"You left it under the bed."

She stared at him like she was barely even on earth anymore and said nothing.

"Why do you have Ivy's phone?" he said.

She took a deep breath. "I think I have to say it now," she said. "I finally have to."

And his stomach twisted with those words, with the finality of them. This was what everything had been leading up to, suddenly he knew that. Maybe all along, it wasn't Steph or secret sadness over some undetermined thing. No, it was *guilt*.

"Did you *steal* her *phone*?" Xavier couldn't process what was happening.

Sasha didn't answer, which was all the answer he needed.

And the events of the last few days started to make a different kind of sense. All the hiding and sneaking around, texting, texting when she thought he couldn't see. *This* was what all of it was about.

"Does Ivy know you have it?" He was starting to feel scared of the way Sasha was looking at him. Or maybe scared of Sasha herself.

Cars zipped by behind her. Sasha didn't answer. Something occurred to him then, something he didn't want to even consider, but he couldn't help it. The text Ivy had sent, the one breaking up with him that hadn't even sounded like her at all. "Have you been ..." Xavier could barely bring himself to ask. "... texting as her?"

Sasha nodded.

Oh my god.

"So when Ivy sent me that text breaking up with me," Xavier said. He was speaking so slowly. "Was that ... you?"

Sasha nodded again.

"But why?" Xavier said.

They stood there, cars rushing by. Xavier wanted time to stop, to freeze in this moment so he didn't have to know what she'd say next, what he'd say next. He didn't want to know what was about to happen.

Ivy's phone buzzed in his hand. Another message popped up on the screen. Gwen again. You haven't written me back in hours. I'm getting worried. . . .

In hours? Sasha was texting Gwen as Ivy, too. Xavier held the phone up so Sasha could see. "Gwen's worried," he said.

"I know," Sasha said. She paused. "And she's right to be."

His heart was pounding so hard. "Why is she right to be worried?"

"Something very bad happened." Her voice broke. It broke and her entire body started shaking. "Something very bad happened to Ivy."

"I don't understand," Xavier said. He felt suddenly very sick.

"Ivy . . ."—Sasha exhaled slowly—"was killed."

But of course the words she was saying weren't true. How could they be true?

"What are you talking about?" Xavier said.

"Ivy is dead," Sasha said. "She was killed in the woods four days ago. I didn't want to have to tell you. I tried my best to protect you. I . . ." Tears were on her cheeks, streaming down her face. "I tried my best not to have you know, to keep it from you. To keep it from everyone. But I can't anymore. I have to tell you what happened."

Xavier's body was freezing cold, then burning hot, and he was outside of time, standing there in that Florida parking lot as Sasha said those words to him, words he could not begin to understand. Xavier just stared and stared, then opened his mouth as a question bubbled up out of him. A question that Xavier wasn't even sure he could bring himself to ask. "Did you . . . ?" he started to say. But Sasha stopped him. She shook her head, took a breath.

"I didn't kill her," Sasha said. She looked him straight in the eye. "You did."

Sasha

Each time I heard myself repeat the story, it seemed less and less possible it could be true. I explained everything, right from the beginning from that first night when I created Jake, up until that moment together in the parking lot.

"I don't understand," he said over and over. "Please tell me again?" And with each retelling his eyes grew wider. He asked question after question. And then the story came back out of him in dribbles and bursts.

You did.

I did.

She did.

You did.

Those pills.

Blacked out.

I almost.

We almost.

We did.

And then she was.

Her body was.

And now she is.

Her body is.

And you.

And I.

All along.

I saw his face change when he finally got it. A second later he ran to the side of the parking lot and began to vomit.

I watched him, didn't follow. Down at the road, trucks zipped past under the bright summer sky. He was a wild-eyed animal. I thought at any moment he might start running—into the woods, into traffic, straight off the edge of the goddamn Earth. Or maybe I'd do it first.

Xavier staggered back. He sat down on the curb, leaned forward, his elbows on his knees and his head in his hands. I looked through the big plate-glass window into the empty lobby. He coughed and spat bile onto the pavement. "This can't be real," he said. But even then, I knew he already understood: things that don't seem possible happen all the time. He looked up at me.

"What happens now?" he said.

"You have to hold it together," I said.

His eyes did not look right. He was about to lose his fucking mind. And once that happened, there would be no going back.

"I don't know if I can," he said.

But of course, we are all capable of both more and less than we ever could have imagined.

"You need to keep it together now, until I figure out what we are going to do next," I said. Only it was already clear what we had to do—it was what I should have done the moment I first found her in the woods. We had to go to the police and turn ourselves in. Both of us.

He was hunched over, shoulders shaking, in a place beyond tears. He slowly turned and looked up at me. "Why did you try to protect me?" he said. "Why did you try to help me? Why did you . . ."

"Because—"I paused. I raised my hand to my chest, pressed a flat palm against my heart. I closed my eyes. I breathed in deep.

I imagined our entire relationship stretching out behind me like rope, thick and strong, going through my chest into the center of me. I thought of all the things I'd wanted to say for so long but was scared to say, what I had convinced myself not to say. I thought of everything that had led up to this moment, the previous weeks, but also months. I thought of Xavier's face, sweetly shy, when he turned toward me in that class our sophomore year and asked if I wanted to team up for a project. I thought of the words that had been sitting hot inside my mouth, about how many times I'd imagined saying them, how desperately I'd wanted to and how scared I'd been to do it. "I was in love with you," I finished.

And suddenly all the racing around stopped. He nodded, then looked at his hands, looked at me. He closed his mouth. Opened it again. "I think I was in love with you, too," he said. "Maybe for a long time, but I was too terrified to admit it even to myself." And I pressed my lips together so no sound could escape.

It was the thing I wanted more than anything in the world. The thing I thought would make me whole. The thing I thought would save me.

"It doesn't matter anymore," I said.

"I know," he said. And he stared out at the road and was silent.

The PROBLEM with STORIES is that only some of them are true. And even if you can tell one that sounds good, sounds VERY BELIEVABLE, even if you MADE IT SEEM like someone was IN THE WOODS who was maybe NOT EVER EVEN THERE it doesn't change what is real, it does not change what ACTUALLY HAPPENED, no matter how much you might want it to.

Once upon a time, there was a girl who found a best friend against all odds. And the best friend was sometimes kind of a terrible person, not ALWAYS but SOMETIMES. But the girl was used to taking what she could get. She was used to taking the scraps and the shit and she did not care about anything anyway. Shit is no different than gold if you don't give a fuck about either.

Let's call the girl Gwen. Let's call her best friend Ivy.

Sasha

Together in that room and nothing was real and we were outside of time and off of Earth. And my brain was ping-ponging around in my skull, as I tried and tried to figure out any way out of this, tried to figure out any answer but the one I kept coming back to.

You can't stop time, I know that. But I tried my very best to pause it.

I told Xavier we would go to the police in the morning and tell them everything, tell them the full truth of what had happened.

We sat in the room in that hotel, on the bed, then lay back, side by side. Not touching. Frozen as the world moved on without us. I did not know how many hours had passed, but when I looked up, it was dark out the window, and it seemed like it would be dark forever.

Ivy was bewitching and greedy. She said she loved Gwen very much, but she didn't always act like it. What good is love that doesn't FEEL like love? That is what Gwen wondered sometimes.

Gwen was Gwen was Gwen was Gwen. What was there to say? Her life was her life, there were sad things and happy things. Gwen was no better or worse than anyone else. Smarter in some ways, but in other ways a real fucking dummy.

One day, Ivy got back together with her ex-boyfriend, Xavier. She MOSTLY DID IT because she SAW him with his BEST FRIEND. Ivy was VERY JEALOUS of that best friend, though she would never admit it. Whatever you had, Ivy would take from you. She only liked things if someone else wanted them. Keep that in mind. That part is important.

Ivy had a tendency to mess things up. She would mess things up with that boyfriend. He was so SOLID and LOYAL and SWEET and THERE. Ivy loved him for it. But she hated him for it, too. Not that Ivy ever said that. Gwen could just tell. HE FUCKED LIKE A FUCKING CHAMPION is what Ivy had said instead.

Having Xavier there to fawn over her distracted Ivy for a full few days, gave her the attention she wanted and craved. She got it from a lot of places usually, like from guys who'd heart-eyes and tongue-out emoji all her Instagram posts and would sometimes start DMing her. She'd let Gwen sign into her account and write them back if Gwen wanted, they were mostly dumb idiots . . . but they were fun and writing to them let Gwen get to see what it would be like to be Ivy and have everybody want you that much. Even in real life, Ivy always sucked up all the love in the room. It didn't make sense, it wasn't FAIR. But anyone who thinks life makes sense or is fair, well you can't even reason with a person like THAT.

Ivy was back with Xavier. And there was Gwen, alone again, alone as EVER.

And then all of a sudden, there was Jake.

HE JUST APPEARED. JUST LIKE MAGIC. He wrote Ivy a message on Instagram. Gwen was WITH her when she got it, Ivy and Gwen were TOGETHER late at night on her ex-now-not-ex-anymore boyfriend's birthday, after Ivy and Xavier had fucked in the woods and Ivy made him take her back. Ivy was forcing Gwen to HEAR about it. Then the message came through. Ivy was like OH GOD ANOTHER ONE. And pretended to be annoyed and handed her phone right over to Gwen, the way she liked to do sometimes. They'd done it before, a million times. Ivy didn't even WRITE ANY of those messages herself.

TAKE IT IF YOU WANT IT, she said, so casual, take IT like he was the last piece of cold pizza and she was already full. But he was NOT pizza or COLD or ANYTHING he was JAKE and he was perfect.

GWEN HAD TO HIDE HOW PERFECT SHE THOUGHT HE WAS.

Ivy was jealous of everyone. But ESPECIALLY, IVY was JEALOUS of ANYONE when it came to Gwen. As in: she didn't want Gwen to have ANYBODY ELSE. And if Gwen ever did, she tried to RUIN it. And even though Gwen KNEW this, it didn't MATTER, it didn't HELP.

On the night Gwen and Jake planned to meet, Gwen was VERY EXCITED. Gwen went to find him at the diner he promised to be at, BUT HE DID NOT SHOW UP. She SAT there and SAT there and thought that maybe he had come in and seen her and

LEFT when he saw her. She was so embarrassed she did not even TEXT him. But then she signed into Ivy's Instagram just in case maybe his PHONE HAD BROKEN and she saw the messages between JAKE and IVY, and suddenly she understood what had happened. She understood what Ivy had done.

Gwen went to the woods. She knew exactly where they would be, it was Ivy's favorite spot. Gwen thought Jake and Ivy would still BE there. But instead Ivy was ALONE. She was ALONE and HIGH with LEAVES in her HAIR, and when she saw Gwen she just said, GWEN, LISTEN, I WAS ONLY EVER TRYING TO PROTECT YOU.

Once upon a time, there was a girl named Gwen who went into the woods and did something terrible by accident, but even if she could, she wouldn't take it back.

Xavier

Xavier sat on the curb outside the hotel alone in the warm, soft dark and tried to picture it. He tried to remember stumbling into those woods, her terrified eyes, her desperate gasps for breath, her body sinking to the ground. The anger he surely must have felt. But all he could see was darkness, like black smoke. All he could feel was the blunted dreamlike terror that he knew hadn't even fully hit him yet, but was coming.

There was relief in forgetting, but Xavier did not deserve to forget.

Sasha had not wanted to let him go outside alone. He knew she was scared of what he might do: throw himself in front of a car or leap off the roof. "I promise I won't do anything stupid," he said. And he wouldn't. He would face whatever was coming for him now.

Sasha had let him borrow her phone. He took it out,

dialed the number, it rang only once, and there she was.

"Hello?" He heard his mother's voice as though for the first time in his life.

"Mom?" he said. "It's me, from Sasha's phone." He stood up. There was another car in the parking lot now.

"Oh, Xavier," she said. His sweet mom, who he knew was so happy to hear from him, even though she would never be able to open up enough to say it. "Are you and Sasha having fun?" Xavier thought she sounded off, then realized it wasn't her who was different. It was him.

"Yeah . . . we're having . . . it's good," he said. She was probably starting to worry by now, and wish he'd come home. She was probably telling herself to just be glad he was out of bed, having a nice time. This is the thing that hurt Xavier the most.

"Please let her mother and her boyfriend know that we're happy to chip in to pay for you, for meals and things. Whatever fun activities you're doing . . ." She tried so hard, to do what was good and what was right. "And please will you thank them for me and Dad?"

"I will," he said. "How are you doing over there?"

"We're good," she said. "Your father is making kebabs tonight."

There was a shuffling sound in the background.

"I love you," Xavier said.

There was a beat of silence. Xavier knew his parents loved

him, but it wasn't something they usually said out loud. Wasn't something they ever said, really.

"I love you, too," she said. "When are you coming back?"

"Soon, Mom," he said. "I have to go now, though."

He hung up the phone and started to cry.

I sat in the parking lot, SAT AND SAT for HOURS and HOURS. SAT in that PARKING LOT of THE MERMAID HIDEAWAY MOTEL, waiting and waiting for someone, but I was not sure WHO. I was not sure if they were even HERE. I had been there now for HOURS just THINKING and THINKING with NO BREAK AT ALL.

My STOMACH HURT because for days I had been eating MOSTLY REST-STOP TAFFY and NO ACTUAL FOOD. I did not know how LONG I would WAIT, because "IVY" had not answered me in a very long time. And had not posted a new picture since first thing that morning and now it was night. I went inside and some creep at the desk stared at me. DO YOU WANT A ROOM? he asked. NO THANK YOU, I said. I AM

WAITING FOR SOMEONE, and he said, WHO? and I said, I AM WAITING FOR IVY!

Just joking. I did not say that. I JUST WENT BACK OUTSIDE AND GOT INTO THE CAR.

I did not tell him who I HOPED I could be waiting for. I barely even told MYSELF. But we all have HOPES don't we—there is nothing wrong with HOPING, IS THERE?

Even at my very sickest, I have always known I'm not actually crazy. I'm maybe TOO SANE, if anything. But I WILL ADMIT something, I will ADMIT IT NOW: when I got that VERY FIRST text from "IVY," for one quarter of one half of one tenth of a second, I actually wondered if I was. Crazy. Because I know for sure only a few things in life, but one of them is this: DEAD GIRLS DON'T TEXT BACK.

So when I got that very first message from "IVY," I stared at my phone and thought, HOW CAN THIS BE? Because she was first DEAD, yet then somehow GONE and now TEXTING?? AND THAT IS JUST NOT HOW THAT WORKS.

Is there a CHANCE I was WRONG about EVERYTHING, maybe she is not even DEAD?

But look, I am no stranger to a DEAD BODY. I was there when my mom died. And also there for the months and months when she was teetering on the edge between dead and alive, so let me tell you: I CAN TELL THE GODDAMNED DIFFERENCE.

So WHO were those messages FROM? I asked myself. And then I thought MAYBE the person who had MADE IT SEEM like someone was DEAD was SENDING TEXTS, was the same as the person who convinced me that ANYTHING MEANT ANYTHING, which is an even BIGGER MAGIC TRICK when you really think about it.

Maybe he came back and saw what was out there in the woods and panicked, took her phone and ran? At first, I was not sure I even wanted to believe that. Because even though I AM a monster, I know that HE is NOT ONE. But then I thought WELL, MAYBE ANYONE can do ANYTHING if they have THE VERY RIGHT REASONS.

So WHO was I WAITING for? I WAS NOT EVEN SURE.

I sat there IN MY CAR, figuring if they came outside, I would see them. I would SEE whoever it WAS and would KNOW. I looked down at my phone. I read through all the text messages Ivy and I had ever sent. The ones from after. The ones from BEFORE. And I started to feel something in my chest that I really did not want to feel at all, SO THEN I STOPPED READING. And right at that moment, I looked up and saw someone walk outside the hotel. Tall and powerful with a swoop of blue at the top.

He sat down on the curb.

I unrolled my window to make sure. JUST TO MAKE SURE.

I could smell the trees and feel the air on my skin and in my lungs and the blood inside me racing around and going into and out of my POUNDING, POUNDING HEART. I could feel FUCKING EVERYTHING.

I got out. I walked toward him.

And suddenly it was like every bad thing that had ever happened before in my life did not matter. Every bad thing I had ever done, every regret I ever had LIFTED, because everything had led me THERE to that moment thousands of miles from home in a near-empty parking lot in the HOT DARK.

I saw who it was, and I knew who it was, and just like that, I understood everything.

Xavier

Xavier didn't hear the car door slam, didn't hear her footsteps, didn't hear her at all until she was right in front of him, staring down. He looked up.

Gwen's eyes were open so wide. For a moment, they just watched each other. She looked like she had not slept in a very long time. He knew he should probably be very surprised to see her, but he also knew maybe he would never be surprised by anything again. A dinosaur could walk out, stomp them all to death. A thirty-foot wave could sweep them all away. It wouldn't somehow feel any different than what had already happened.

The thing was, what was he supposed to *do* now that she was here, standing in front of him, looking down like he might have answers?

He wished Sasha would come outside and tell him what

to do. But no, he did not get that luxury. He did not deserve it.

He was going to have to tell Gwen himself.

Oh God, he was going to have to tell her what he had done.

"Listen—" he started.

But she cut him off. "It was you," she said, halfway between asking and telling. She was shaking her head slowly.

And Xavier realized then that somehow she already knew her best friend was dead—and that Xavier had done it. How did she know? He did not wonder why. He did not wonder how. Because nothing in this entire world made sense or ever had or ever would. But he understood at least that much.

"Yes," Xavier said. He wanted to qualify it with something. He wanted to say that he didn't even remember, and that he was sorry. How he was so, so, so fucking sorry. But the words didn't mean enough. Nothing meant anything. "It was me," he said. "I did it."

She shook her head again. Her mouth was a perfect round O.

"All along, it never even occurred to me to think, or dream . . ." Her face started to transform bit by bit. The corners of her mouth curled up into an expression that made so little sense, Xavier could not even tell what it was at first. A smile. She was smiling. Her smile spread and spread.

She crouched down beside him on the curb where he sat. She reached one hand up and touched his cheek. He could barely feel it. What was happening? "It all makes sense now," she said.

She leaned toward him. Leaned in close. She smelled like sweat and unwashed skin and sour breath. She raised her hand to her lips and tipped her head to the side.

"Oh, honey," she said. "I'm sorry. Your face—you look so confused. I should explain. . . . Xavier, the person you were texting with, it wasn't her, it wasn't Ivy. . . ." She paused. Xavier felt like maybe something was wrong with his brain and he'd forgotten what words meant, because he did not understand at all. Gwen kept going.

"Obviously she didn't tell you about me, just like she didn't tell me about you. It would have driven her *insane*, her best friend and her boyfriend. In some fucked-up way, it makes sense, right? I guess she would rather . . ."—Gwen paused— "would have rather you thought she was going to cheat than have you know you connected with her best friend in a way you'd never connected with her."

Xavier was stuck in a dream. He could not understand any of the words she was saying, or why she was smiling when her best friend was dead. Why was she reaching out her hand toward the person who had killed her?

"I was so angry at her in those woods," Gwen said. "I mean so *angry*, but now I realize I should be grateful that this is where we ended up."

He could not understand why she was then wrapping her arms around him, and he wanted to pull away, but he could not get his body to move at all.

She leaned back. Her face was changing. She was starting to look scared. "Please say something," she said. "I know this is a lot to take in, but just please say you're not mad at me. You have to understand, it was an accident, honestly, and the thing with your hairs in her hand . . . When I did that . . . I was just trying to make a story look true! And I had her house key and her brush was *right there* and there was so much blue in it. . . . I had *no idea* you were Jake. It never even occurred to me. I'm so sorry. But please don't be mad. We're the same, you and me . . . and we're in this together now. . . ."

She was staring at him. He realized that she wanted something from him, and that she was very desperate to get it. She had a hand on each of his shoulders, and still nothing made any sense. "I just need to know though: Why did you move her? And why all the texting?"

He felt, in the back of his head, something uncurling. Making him realize that he understood even less than he thought he did.

"Were you trying to protect me? But you didn't know it was me. Did you? Remember what you said right at the beginning? About how in a parallel world maybe we are already in love? Well, maybe you could think about that, how happy we are, how . . ." Her words were coming faster and faster, she sounded like she was running out of air.

Running out of air.

"Holy shit," Gwen said. She pulled away. She was looking

at something behind him. Xavier turned. There was Sasha, rais-
ing her hand to her lips.

Gwen stood.

Sasha opened her mouth. When she spoke, her voice was a
whisper. "But parallel worlds are no kinder than this one. . . ."

Time slowed down. Gwen and Sasha stared at each other.
They stepped in closer.

Sasha

I reached for something to steady myself, grasped at the air. The world kept shifting and shifting and spinning, and there was nothing I nor anyone could do to stop it.

We stayed there like that, eyes locked. I understood then, just what had happened. We had shared something impossible and unimaginable, dangerous and destructive, shared something no one else on earth would ever truly understand.

And right then, against all reason, for one single moment, as I looked at her, the only thing in my head and in my heart was this:

You made me feel less alone.

There was the sound of crying—Xavier was crying. I turned away.

Xavier hadn't killed her.

He hadn't done anything I thought he had.

And Gwen had done it all.

And everything came flooding back: Why we were there, how we had gotten there, what I thought had happened, what had actually happened. What we hadn't done, and what we had.

What both of us fucking had.

And what I had to do next.

I was TEETERING on the EDGE of what was HAPPEN-ING, and I could NOT really BEAR it, it was TOO MUCH to BEAR. I HAD MADE A HORRIBLE FUCKING MIS-TAKE. I HAD MADE SO MANY. AND NOW I NEEDED HELP.

But there was no one to help.

MOTHERS lift CARS if their CHILD is TRAPPED UNDER-NEATH. If someone TRULY LOVES you, they will DO ANY-THING to KEEP YOU SAFE. I was the kid trapped under the car, but I was also the mother too. I HAD TO BE. Because there was no one on earth who could save me, who would try, who would want to. NO ONE EXCEPT FOR ME.

And I started to piece together WHY they had DONE some very CONFUSING THINGS. It was because SOMEHOW, both of them thought certain other things had ACTUALLY HAPPENED though I did not yet understand HOW. And Sasha was holding a phone, fingers starting to dial. Nine, then one, about to press the other FINAL ONE. And I felt a rush and my entire body was overtaken by quiet calm:

Even though NOTHING MATTERED, I still cared about what happened. MAYBE I CARED ABOUT MYSELF MORE THAN I THOUGHT.

I told Sasha to stop dialing.

And she stopped. Of course she did.

I may be stupid ABOUT MOST THINGS, it turned out. And there were MANY THINGS I did not understand yet, would not fully grasp until later, but even in that moment I knew this: I knew how much Sasha loved Xavier, how much Xavier loved her back. It was obvious since that very first night I saw them at Sloe Joe's, before everything that was going to happen happened. And I knew love made them weak. I knew it made them willing to do anything. Just like it had made me.

Soon I would understand more of their secrets, and they would understand more of mine. But not this one, not ever this one:

When my EYES met JAKE'S, the real Jake's, I felt something deep in my heart. The feelings I had before when we first started writing and kept writing and kept writing, THEY WERE ALL STILL THERE, and if she had wanted to try, to try to do everything we said, everything we promised to each other late at night, even now that I knew who she actually was . . . I would have tried it. Even after everything.

That is my secret. I have many now. I will never be free of them. But maybe that is the worst one of all. She turned away first. Jake turned away first. But if she hadn't turned away?

I think I never would have.

Xavier

Everything after that happened so fast.

Xavier could barely breathe, and then that was all he could do, terror and grief and relief swirling together inside of him.

Ivy was dead.

He hadn't killed her.

But she was still dead.

There they were, the three of them, so very far from home. So much had led up to this moment that he didn't understand yet, wouldn't understand for a long time. Only one thing was clear: This wasn't over. Maybe it never would be.

Time slowed down. Then sped up.

And the bubble popped and the trance was broken. And Xavier was crying, because it was all really, truly starting to sink in. The Ivy Xavier had known was not on this planet anymore. She was a mix of dark and light, of sweet and terrible, of flawed and perfect. There would never be anyone quite like her ever again. And she was gone.

But the three of them were still there. Gwen and Sasha had inched closer, then stepped back. Sasha's hands were curled into tight, dirty fists, and Gwen's face had changed, like a door had snapped shut behind her eyes.

And she shook her head, slowly, blinking, as though she was just then figuring something out. Gwen turned toward Xavier. Her voice sounded totally different than before. "When you said 'it was me, I did it,' you really did believe . . ."

Sasha reached out and took the phone from Xavier's hand. "It doesn't matter now," Sasha said quickly. She started to dial. The 9, then the 1, then before she dialed the last 1 . . .

"No, I guess it actually doesn't," Gwen said. "But unless you want your friend to go to jail for a very long time, I'd put the phone down. . . ."

Sasha froze. "He didn't do anything."

"So what? The important thing is what it seems like. And you of all people should fucking know that. *Anything can look true.*" Gwen shrugged. "Besides, you pretended to be her and moved her body. Neither of you are getting out of this. Guess we're all in this together now. So what are we going to do about it?"

Xavier felt himself starting to sink. He didn't care what happened to him. Not really, not anymore. But as Sasha and Gwen circled each other, one thought stood out in Xavier's mind. One thing he couldn't forget and never would: Sasha had only ever wanted to protect him. She had done a lot of crazy things, some truly crazy things and he so desperately wished that she hadn't, but he understood why.

When you love someone, you will do anything to keep them safe.

And now it was his turn.

"Listen," Xavier said as he stood. His slow brain switched back on, and started working very quickly. They looked up at him, like they were surprised to hear his voice at all. He knew what they had to do. It was obvious and easy and insane and terrible. It was not a perfect plan, and maybe it wouldn't work, and it certainly wouldn't work forever. But it was their only chance and maybe it had been Sasha's plan all along. Maybe that's why she'd been texting as Ivy, updating Instagram as Ivy. Maybe. They hadn't discussed it, and now he knew they never would. It would work far better now with Gwen than it ever could have without her. Gwen was the final missing piece.

You can't buy innocence, you can only buy time. And at least it would give them that. Who knows how much any of us have anyway?

Xavier took a breath. "Here's what's going to happen."

August 13, 10:36 p.m.

Gwen: Where are you now?

Ivy: At the Everglades

Gwen: when are you coming back?

Ivy: Not sure . . . He says he wants to stay here for a while

Gwen: I still don't know who HE is, you haven't told me

Ivy: Of course you do. He's the one I met that night in the city after you went home

Gwen: wait THAT guy? Do you even know his last name?

Ivy: NOPE.

Gwen: Ivy that is insane even for you

Ivy: Psssh. Don't be jealous

Gwen: and you're camping? You hate camping

Ivy: We're having fun, it's okay. I said I wanted to maybe stay in a hotel but he got kind of weird about it and I don't have any money, so it's whatever

Gwen: weird about it how?

Ivy: I have to go, he'll be back soon.

Gwen: so what?

Gwen: Hello?

Gwen: Ivy???

Ivy: he gets jealous

Gwen: I'm calling you

Gwen: I called you

Gwen: Ivy?

Ivy: don't worry. Just don't call again

Gwen: you're scaring me now, where are you?

Ivy: oh god calm down . . . what are you, my fucking mother? I'm in the same place as before

Gwen: tell him you want to come back . . . or leave

Ivy: Stop being so dramatic, I'm having fun

Gwen: Ivy COME BACK I'm serious. I don't think this is good . . . should I call your mom?

Ivy: NO. Jesus. Don't you dare. I will never speak to you again and I will get in so much trouble. Everything is FINE.

Gwen: What do you guys even do all day?

Ivy: Mostly we just hang out. . . . He wants us to go on a hike tomorrow

Gwen: you hate hiking

Ivy: guess I'm learning a lot about myself. Haha

Gwen: Have fun I guess

Ivy: Thanks. Anyway he's back I have to go.

Gwen: But WHY?

Ivy: he doesn't like me texting too much

Gwen: I'm your best friend

Ivy: Of course. But don't text again. And don't tell anyone. I'll see you when I get back, okay?

Gwen: When will that be?

Gwen: Ivy?

1 year later

She is sitting in a booth at the diner when Xavier walks in. He turns like he's looking for her, even though she knows that can't be true, shouldn't be true. They do not talk anymore, they haven't in a long time.

They lock eyes. Neither waves, but something passes between them. It's his eighteenth birthday.

"Babe?" Her boyfriend Steph touches her hand from across the table. "Are you done?" The server is waiting to take her plate.

"Oh, sorry," Sasha says. "Yes, I am."

It took five weeks for them to find the body.

Sasha had been waiting in line at a gas station when the news finally broke. She saw the report on the TV behind the register. She forced herself to breathe. She finished paying. Then went into the bathroom and threw up.

A man had been illegally fishing in that lake, caught something heavier than a fish on his hook, tugged and tugged, and then pulled up a whirl of dark hair that looked human. He wasn't surprised, he said on the news. "If I was going to dump a body, this is where I'd do it."

A year has passed since all of this began. Sasha tries her best not to think about Ivy. But Ivy's always there, simmering at the back of her awareness with every heartbeat.

Steph is holding Sasha's hand now. He smiles at her, big and bright. They are both heading off to college in the fall. He wants to stay together, but in her mind they have already broken up and she is long gone. But also part of her will never leave this place, will never leave the lake and the woods. Nothing will ever change. But already some things are so different.

Up at the counter, Xavier is still watching her. Eighteen, an adult now. And a child and a boy and a baby and no one. And no longer her best friend, but her first love, her true love. Her still love. And he always will be. Sasha stares at him. She was not his first, but she is the one who made him whole and the one who broke him.

It matters, but it doesn't.

They are all so good at pretending now.

When the police found the body, Gwen came forward.

She's the only one who knew much of anything, it seemed. She told the police first, and then later anyone who would listen: about the guy Ivy had met while the two of them were out one night, how Gwen didn't think much of it at the time, because with Ivy, there was always someone. They were in the city and it was dark and Gwen never really got a good look at him. Ivy said he was super persistent—she never even gave him her phone number, just told him where she lived and where she went to summer school, and he kept showing up. He took Ivy on a road trip. Ivy texted Gwen the whole way, at least at first. And then Ivy stopped texting. And Gwen got a little worried, but she didn't tell anyone. She didn't want her best friend to get in trouble. She was only ever trying to protect her. And then Ivy's body was found. And there was an investigation.

It is open and ongoing. No one has turned up anything so far.

Gwen stopped going to school after that. There are rumors that she missed Ivy so much she tried to kill herself. There are rumors she did too many drugs and got sent to rehab. There are rumors she had something to do with Ivy's death, and went on the run. But no one really believes that. Hardly anyone, really.

Sasha, Xavier, Gwen, the three of them are tied together forever, tied so tightly they will never truly be rid of each other.

They've made their choices, and there is nothing left to do but live with them the best they can.

Xavier turns away now. He hasn't moved from the counter. Sasha thinks for a moment that maybe he is alone on his birthday. And something happens in her heart. She feels herself starting to stand. And she thinks maybe she will go over to him. Maybe they can start again, or pretend just for today that that is even possible. But, no. No. She sits back down as Xavier's parents walk up behind him.

Steph gives her hand a squeeze. "What do you want to do this afternoon?" he says. "A movie and then the dog park?" He is good. Sweet and kind. A solid, honest person. She does not deserve him. She probably does not deserve anything. But she will take it anyway. She is a monster, but maybe everyone is. Or could be.

Ivy's body had decayed by the time she was found. That was the word that stuck with Sasha from the report: decayed. You hear a word like that and you can't help but picture it, you can't help but picture what warm water does to soft skin when it is left soaking for far too long and longer still, grows spongy and starts to peel away.

It was national news, a big, splashy front-page story. Everyone loves a pretty dead girl, and to be reminded of what happens to girls who aren't careful.

There's a message board in an online forum now, devoted

to Ivy. It's mostly used by conspiracy theorists, armchair detectives, and lonely, horny men who have fallen in love with Ivy's picture, the same way they always did when she was alive. Sasha used to read the board sometimes, until one day someone started posting too many things that were too close to the truth. Their username was ParallelWorlds. They wrote in manic bursts late at night. They sounded, sometimes, unhinged. Sasha stopped looking after that.

The police are still searching for the man Ivy had met out one night in the dark, and who knows what they will find. The truth always comes to the surface, that's what Sasha believes. It always comes to the surface.

Except when it doesn't.

Xavier is picking up their order now. His mother is paying. His father is getting extra ketchup, extra napkins. They are walking out.

Sasha and Xavier will leave this town behind soon and try not to look back. She still loves him. She will always love him. Her love is pure and frozen in time. But love is dangerous.

Where do we hide the secrets we keep? Lodged in our bellies, in our chests, in our throats?

Xavier looks at Sasha one more time before he steps through the door. When their eyes meet, she wants to smile, but she doesn't. Their faces show no expression. And then he is gone.

She tells herself maybe somehow, one day, they will find their way back to each other. In the future, in some other life, they will find their way back home to each other. She pretends to believe it.

She will have to pretend forever now.

ACKNOWLEDGMENTS

Many people helped with this book, and I am hugely grateful. Thank you so much to:

My wonderful editor and friend, Liesa Abrams Mignogna, for being endlessly brilliant, kind, patient, funny, and fun. I feel so lucky to get to work with you.

The excellent people at Simon & Schuster, including: Mara Anastas, Mary Marotta, Catherine Hayden, fantastic publicist Jodie Hockensmith, Christina Pecorale, Gary Urda, Karen Lahey, Victor Iannone and the rest of the sales team, Katherine Devendorf, Sarah Creech, Sara Berko, Jennifer Rothkin, and Ian Reilly. Extra-special thanks to the delightful Jessica Smith for the invaluable editorial feedback and notes.

The marvelous Regina Flath for the stunning US cover.

My incredible agent, Jenny Bent, for everything, including: brainstorming, advice giving, being hilarious, and all the help along the way.

The amazing team at The Bent Agency, especially: Victoria Lowes, Sam Brody, John Bowers, and Molly Ker Hawn. And extra-special thanks to the lovely Nicola Barr.

My fabulous UK editor, Stella Paskins. And the team at Egmont Electric Monkey: Alice Hill, Samuel Perrett (for the gorgeous UK cover and interiors), Anna Robinette, and Amy St Johnston.

My wonderful parents, Cheri Weingarten and Donald Weingarten!

My great pals who helped: Melanie Altarescu, Sarah Rees Brennan, Brendan Duffy, Adele Griffin, Brent Hagen, Micol Ostow Harlan, Aaron Lewis, Michael Northrop, Dan Poblocki, Siobhan Vivian, and Melissa Walker. Extra thanks and ice cream sandwiches to Robin Wasserman for, among many other things, the enormously smart notes. To Lee Overtree for discussing every aspect of this book over one million times and having excellent suggestions all along the way. To Mary Crosbie (and Whiskers!) for the last-minute read to make sure it all made sense.

And thank you so much to anyone who has taken the time to read this book. And even the acknowledgments. All the way to the bottom!